The Adrian Account

A Tony Taylor Adventure

Bob Means

High Tide
Publications, Inc.
It's never too late to write

Published by High Tide Publications, Inc.
www.Hightidepublications.com
Deltaville, Virginia

Edited by Carol J. Bova

Book design by Firebellied Frog Graphic Design

Prologue

A reporter from the *San Francisco Herald* sat between Lefty and me at the empty bar in Tony Nik's. Lefty's scars were still fresh from the beating he'd taken in the Inalco tower basement.

The reporter looked at his notes, "You two were working for Janet LeGrand, owner of LeGrand Gallery, to contact Eva Braun in Argentina to halt the sales of stolen Nazi art through the gallery?"

"That's right," I nodded.

"One of the pieces belonged to Francois Meyer, a French Jew whose parents were executed in Auschwitz?"

I nodded again.

"Francois Meyer was part of the mission?"

I glanced at the reporter. "Yes."

The reporter looked at Lefty. "You were snow skiing with three German girls in Bariloche, Argentina, when two men emerged and separated you from your friends. They muscled you down the slope with a gun in your back, forced you into a van, and then what happened?"

Lefty exhaled smoke from his Camel, squinted his eyes, and raised his beer bottle toward the mirror on the back of the bar.

"They stuck a needle in my arm."

"They drugged you?"

"Yeah, man, they drugged me," said Lefty as he took a drink from his bottle.

"What happened after that? Did you go out cold?"

"No, man, I went into fairy book land. I knew what was happening; they put me on this boat, but I couldn't do anything about it."

Scribbling on his notepad, "Did they tie you up before they put you in the boat?"

"They tied my hands and feet to a cleat on the side of the boat."

"Where did they take you?"

"I don't know. I kept going in and out of consciousness until we tied up at this other dock."

"It was the tower on Lake Nahuel Huapi where Hitler's guards watched for incoming traffic," I added.

"Thank you, Mr. Taylor, but I need Lefty to answer these questions. I'll get to you later."

Lefty looked at the reporter and answered with a snarl, "It was the tower. Hitler's guards watched for incoming traffic."

"Okay, you were tied to a chair in some kind of dungeon, and they began abusing you."

"You can say that. They beat my face in with their fists."

"Do you remember what they were demanding?"

"They wanted to know about our relationship with this chick, Ursula."

"The daughter of Eva Braun, the wife of Adolf Hitler?"

"I guess so," answered Lefty.

"Why didn't you tell them?"

"Because they were beating my head in, and it pissed me off. I wasn't going to give them shit!"

The reporter paused, writing furiously in his notebook.

"One quick question for you, Mr. Taylor. How did you know where to find Lefty?"

"Through François, we worked with a Jewish underground group with good intel."

"When you and your team began firing on the escaping boat, you weren't afraid of wounding or killing Lefty?"

"Very afraid," I answered. "But we had no other choice. Our main mission was to get this guy, Bender."

"And one of the men in the boat began firing back at you?"

"That's right, that's how Jacob got killed."

"Jacob was with the underground?'

"That's right," I answered.

"After Francois picked you up and you gave chase to the damaged boat, you were shocked to see Lefty at the helm?"

"Very shocked, even more shocked that he started firing at us with a machine pistol!"

Turning to Lefty, "Two questions. Why did you fire on your rescuers, and how did you end up on the helm?"

"Wigged out, man! I didn't know who these fucking people were shooting everything up. I just did it. Is that so hard to understand!" Lefty angrily answered.

Looking down at his notes, the reporter sheepishly asked, "How did you end up on the helm?"

Lefty took a long drag off his Camel, then three gulps of beer. "This kraut dropped dead next to me. He had a knife in his belt. I worked my way around, took the knife, and cut myself free. This Bender, everybody calls him, was trying to get everything out of this shot-up boat. I came up behind him and cut his throat."

"You killed Bender?"

"That's right, man, I cut his goddamn throat."

The *San Francisco Herald* reporter closed his book. "Well, gentlemen, thank you for your time. You sure had an adventure!" He hopped down from his barstool. "I have what I need for now. Here's my card. Don't hesitate to call if you have something else to add."

I briefly looked at the card; Lefty let it lie on the bar and looked at himself in the mirror behind it. Neither of us said goodbye.

After several steps, the reporter turned back. "By the way, did Janet Legrand get the rendezvous with Eva Braun?"

"From what we understand," I answered.

"Did Francois get back his artwork?"

"I don't know."

"One more question for you, Mr. Taylor. Is it true Miss LeGrand had to extort you to get you to go on this mission?"

I turned away from the reporter, finished my Jack Daniels, and lit a cigarette, staring at the mirror.

Realizing he wouldn't get an answer, the reporter turned and left.

Jim, the barkeep, overheard the conversation and brought Lefty another beer, "This one's on the house."

You can tell from the conversation with the reporter that we had a tough time with it. It all started back in 1943 during the Second World War. To the best of my knowledge, here is how it began.

Chapter 1

On January 23, 1943, Doctor Joseph Meyer and his wife, Priscilla, were asleep upstairs in their home in Marseille, France. The house was high enough on the Calanques foothills to glimpse the Mediterranean Sea.

Life was difficult in these troubled times. Having a carefree social life was impossible. The Meyers' 10-year-old son, Francois, had trouble keeping friends.

Dr. Meyer loved collecting art, especially paintings. Because of his heritage, he focused on Jewish artists. His most prized piece was *The Swan* by Marc Chagall, valued at 110,000 French francs. The painting hung over the bronzed mantel in the sitting room.

At 2 a.m., a slight mist wetted the streets. Francois lay peacefully across the hall from his parents' bedroom. Joseph and Priscilla woke up when a car abruptly stopped in front of their home. Headlights shone in their windows. They knew what it meant when they heard approaching footsteps and a loud pounding on the front door. La Milice, the Vichy French militia, had come to collect them and send them to a German concentration camp.

They arose, quickly dressing as the pounding continued. The shout, «Ouvrez-vous; Milice!"

Socks on his feet, buckling his trousers, Joseph ran to the door to stall them as Priscilla rushed into Francois's room. She shook him out of bed and made it up madly as if no one had slept.

She was nervous but did not want Francois to know. She smiled at her son and fastened the collar of his warm coat.

"You know what to do. It's cold outside. Keep your coat buttoned up. Your father and I will meet you soon, don't wait for us!"

"Yes, Mother," Francois answered as he entered the secret escape hatch his father had built and looked back at his mother.

Her hand lingered on the closed hatch. She heard his voice.

"Mother, I'm scared."

She knew this could be the last time she saw her son. She urged him, "Francois, go on, don't stop!"

The last words she heard from her son were, "I love you, Mother."

Francois never saw his parents again.

Chapter 2

Janet LeGrand sat at her desk in the San Francisco LeGrand art gallery twenty years later. She abhorred administration; her passion was sharing her love of art with clients. Clients loved her. Her sultry nature and childhood innocence drove the men crazy, and her charm and culture from a privileged childhood made other women want to be her or protect her from the world. Today, she wasn't in the office to share her passion, but just the opposite.

Lying in front of her was a stack of death certificates she was sending off to various agencies, informing them of her father's death and her subsequent ownership of LeGrand Galleries. She noticed the brown envelope from the *Office of Strategic Services,* which her father had placed in a coiled letter holder years ago. She couldn't remember how far back the letter sat there unopened. She was toying with the sealed envelope when the phone rang.

"LeGrand Galleries," she answered.

"My name is Dieter Hauptmann, and I'm calling from Europe for Madam Janet LeGrand."

She recognized a strong German accent and the familiar delay of an overseas call.

"This is Janet LeGrand, Mr. Hauptmann. How can I help you?"

She waited for the delayed response before reaching him.

"First, Miss LeGrand, I wish to give my heartfelt condolences for the loss of your parents."

She was confused about how Mr. Hauptmann knew about her parents' death since her brother Henry just finished writing their parent's obituary, and it wasn't in the paper yet, but she continued the conversation.

"Thank you very much. It is a great loss, and your condolences are much appreciated. How can I help you, sir?"

"I'm calling regarding the Adrian account. A shipment will arrive from Europe in your New York gallery shortly."

She hesitated. She'd never heard of the Adrian account, and no packages from Europe were scheduled. Although she was acquainted with her father's dealings, this was new.

She didn't want to sound ignorant and said, "Thank you, Mr. Hauptmann. The galleries will close for a month. My parents' sudden death requires a reorganization. Your package will be in storage. As soon as we reopen, it will be our highest priority."

"Miss LeGrand, I understand your situation, and it pains me to have this conversation during your time of loss, but you must expedite this shipment; it can't be delayed. We can postpone our normal interactions until the gallery reopens."

"Mr. Hauptmann, I'm not familiar with your account. I will need a week to sort out the details."

"Miss LeGrand, this is more time-sensitive than a normal transaction. The need is greater than most as lives are at stake."

Stunned by the response and needing time to acquaint herself with this new twist, she said, "Again, sir, I'm unfamiliar with the Adrian account. It will take time before we can respond to your order."

"Miss LeGrand!" he shouted. "You must understand the level of importance of this shipment. Your lack of action could cause the death of other people!"

Realizing this conversation was out of her element, she panicked, "I'm sorry, Mr. Hauptmann, I'll look into it and get back to you as soon as I can."

She hung up without waiting for a response.

It took her a moment to calm down. Picking up her father's death certificate, she wondered, *Is this what it's like working in the office, Dad?*

You were always on top of everything and made it look so easy. I guess I could never appreciate what you did until now.

She sighed as she set down the certificate and stared into the distance. She leaned back in her chair, looking for anything to do to get her mind off the stressful situation; she picked up the brown envelope. It looked old and was postmarked from over fifteen years ago. She sliced open the aging envelope, unfolded the two-page letter, and read:

> *Dear Mr. LeGrand, be aware that the list of paintings on page two is artwork stolen by the Nazi Government that must be returned to its original owners. If you encounter any of these pieces in your transactions, please immediately contact us at the phone number and address below.*
>
> *Sincerely, Bill Donovan*
>
> *Director, Office of Strategic Services*

She scanned the list of artworks on page two. What caught her eye was the fourth item from the top, *The Swan.... Artist, Marc Chagall.*

She returned the letter to the envelope and went to the filing cabinet where her father kept track of his transactions. Opening the drawer to files A through D, she fingered the A folders and could not find the Adrian account file.

Her mind raced, opening every drawer in the cabinet, looking in the desk drawers and every other cranny. She slapped her hip in frustration and wondered, *Why can't I find this account?*

She looked through the window at the darkness outside. It was late. Too upset to do more work, she put on her coat and placed her purse over her shoulder. She reached for the light switch, hesitated, and returned to her desk to pick up the OSS letter. Fearing potential complications, she scanned the bookcase. A book featuring Marc Chagall stood out. Opening the book, she found *The Swan*, inserted the letter, and then placed the book on the coffee table to keep it fresh in her mind.

Unable to shake her anxiety from the turn of events, she turned off the lights, locked the office door, and walked to the stairs leading to the parking garage.

Standing next to her pink Cadillac, she nervously searched inside her purse and said aloud, "Where are those damn keys? I had them when I locked the office door."

Frustrated, she emptied the purse on the hood of her car. The keys did not surface. She stood straight and paused. *Where did I put my keys?*

At the end of the dimly lit garage, she noticed a man sitting behind the wheel of a black sedan, staring at her. It was too dark to see his face, but his angular features and fedora were highlighted as he took a drag off his cigarette. Alarmed, she slid her hand into her coat pocket and pulled out the keys.

Frantically, she shoved the items from the hood into her purse. Too afraid to look up, she unlocked the car door, slid behind the wheel, and fitted the key into the ignition.

She started the car, turned on the headlights, and began to back up. The black sedan's lights came on. As she drove out of the garage, the car pulled up behind her so closely that the headlights in the rearview mirror nearly blinded her. Unnerved, she made a hard right turn.

"What is this idiot doing?" she screamed.

The car stayed on her tail. Increasingly nervous, she made a sharp left turn. It was still there. As she sank into panic mode, she headed directly for the police station.

When she pulled into the police parking lot, the car raced away.

She wondered, *Should I go in and make a report? The police might think I am crazy for reporting someone tailgating me.*

Feeling paranoid, she headed home. No one followed.

Uneasily, she settled into her upstairs condominium. With tangled thoughts, she poured a glass of Merlot. She twisted the cork between her fingers and looked across Bay Street to the San Francisco Harbor. Taking a drink to calm herself, she pulled salad fixings from the fridge while sipping her wine.

As she ate, the wine began to ease the tension. *I'll figure it out in the morning.*

She showered and slipped between the sheets. Before laying her head on the pillow, she opened the drawer on the bedside table, retrieved a thirty-two caliber Beretta, and slid it under the pillow next to her.

Suddenly awake, half sure she heard something, she noticed a light coming from the kitchen.

Did I leave a light on? Thinking again, *I didn't leave a light on.*

Fighting off panic, she reached under the pillow. Squeezing the pistol handle, she placed her finger on the trigger.

"Is anybody here!?" she screamed.

No answer. No sound.

Fear gripped her. She had to check it out. Frantically throwing back the sheets, she sat on the edge of the bed.

"I've got a gun, and I won't hesitate to blow your head off!" she screamed again.

For a moment, she stood next to the bedroom door listening intently... No sounds.

With the pistol in hand, she slowly looked around to the kitchen. The refrigerator door was open, casting a sliver of light across the room.

Did I leave the refrigerator open?

Turning on the kitchen light, she inched forward to close the fridge when She noticed writing on yellow notebook paper inside and froze.

She extracted the exposed letter, shaking so badly she could hardly make out what it said.

"Work on the Adrian account must resume immediately. Lives depend on it, including your own."

She dropped to her knees and leaned back against the sink cabinet, reading the note repeatedly. *What is this?*

Gun in hand, she closed the fridge and checked the rest of the house. She caught her breath when she spied out the front door. It was slightly ajar. Somebody had come in through the front door.

I never leave it unlocked. Somebody has a key. She racked her brain, "Who in God's name has a key to my house?" she said aloud.

She slammed the door shut, relocked it, and placed a chair under the knob. Utterly confused and scared, she picked up the phone and dialed her brother Henry. Henry always knew what to do.

Chapter 3

In 1911, Janet's father, Robert LeGrand, a handsome, gregarious Frenchman, was a budding artist. He met Alice Hopkins from New York. They studied together in the same art studio in Paris. They spent time together, fell in love, and married.

Frustrated by trying to pay the bills by selling his art, Robert became pragmatic. He realized there was more money in dealing with art than producing it. With a small inheritance from his grandfather, he and Alice opened LeGrand Gallery on a back street in Paris.

The couple Invited friends to hang their work on the walls, and before long, they established a robust business. From its humble start, they reinvested and bought pieces from renowned artists, which brought a higher echelon of clients and their wallets into the gallery.

The First World War began in 1914. Uninterested in combat, Robert and Alice packed up their artwork and closed the gallery to take the steamer to New York. Alice's family helped them find a studio in Greenwich Village, where they reopened the LeGrand Gallery.

In 1917, Alice gave birth to a boy named Henry. As their family grew, the gallery catered to the rich and famous. If Robert did not have the right piece for the client, he found it and negotiated the sale. His reputation grew. Serious collectors worldwide contacted Robert to sell or buy art.

Burgeoning sales allowed them to open a second LeGrand Gallery in San Francisco. Between the First and Second World Wars, with LeGrand Galleries on both coasts, their art empire grew far beyond what they ever imagined. Robert and Alice traveled coast to coast and took buying trips to Europe for ever-changing and fresh exhibits.

On a buying trip to Southern France, Robert met an art dealer who invited him to Berlin to meet the artist and rising political stars Adolph Hitler and Eva Braun. Robert was smitten by Eva and taken in by this charismatic man. Their conversations centered on the glories of art. He could not help being impressed as he followed Hitler's rise to power.

Shortly before hostilities broke out in Europe, Robert returned from a buying trip in Europe, and told Alice about a beautiful orphaned baby girl he learned about from a client and wished to add to the family. After lengthy discussions, they adopted this girl and named her Janet.

With the Nazi occupation of France in 1940, the Vichy French became the government. Robert LeGrand sided with the Vichy when they made him an offer he could not refuse. With the arrests and relocations of Jewish families, the Nazis collected a massive amount of confiscated art. Hitler demanded that artwork be brought to him and evaluated for his personal museum.

Hitler's hatred for modern and cubic art allowed pieces that escaped the burn pile to come on the market. A shady curator connected to the Vichy government had connections to warehouses full of contraband art. He enlisted Robert to establish secret pipelines to sell illicit pieces of artwork to discreet buyers.

As the Second World War wound down, the SS leadership realized their crimes against humanity carried a death sentence. With the collaboration of the Vatican, the SS organized escape routes, known as the *Rat Line*, to South America. Sales of stolen art financed these moves and provided an income once they got there. Robert LeGrand was at the hub of these transactions.

International art flooding the market did not go unnoticed as the ovens in concentration camps were burning red hot. President Roosevelt, aware of the pillage of family treasures, commissioned Bill Donovan, head of the OSS, to investigate. Donovan set up the Monuments, Fine Arts, and Archive Division, also known as the Monument Men.

After the war, Robert maintained his membership in the Nazi movement, now operating in South America. His business hit a crescendo he could not hide. The Monument Men had begun to move in on him when he and Alice died in a car crash as they returned to San Francisco from a gala in Sacramento.

Chapter 4

Henry was in a deep sleep when the phone rang. He fumbled for it, try to be certain it wasn't a dream. *Who the hell would call at this ungodly hour!*

"Henry! My house was broken into!" Janet screamed on the phone.

Awakened from a dead sleep, his brain was in a fog. "What? Broke into your house!"

"I'm scared. Something weird is going on."

Henry perked up and sat on the edge of the bed, "What's weird? Tell me what happened."

"I went to bed; a noise woke me up. I got up. The fridge door was open with a note saying, *The Adrian account must resume immediately. Lives depend on it, including your own.*"

"The Adrian account? What in the hell is the Adrian account?"

"That's what I'm trying to figure out. I received this horrid phone call from Europe saying I had to process this painting immediately for the Adrian account. He started yelling at me when I told him he'd have to wait. I hung up on him. I left the office and was followed home. Then later I found this note in the fridge. When I checked the front door, it was ajar. Somebody has a key. What should I do?!!"

"Are you home now, and do you still have the gun I gave you?"

"Yes, I'm home and have the gun. I never thought I would have to use it."

"Listen, do exactly what I tell you: bar the door and dress. I'll call Buck and have him come to your house. He'll escort you to the office, and I'll meet you there as soon as possible."

"I knew you'd know what to do."

"I don't know what to do, but we must start somewhere."

Chapter 5

Clyde Buchanan, known as Buck, was chivalrous to a fault. A Marine veteran from World War II, he was LeGrand Gallery's security agent. He stood six feet tall, weighed two hundred forty pounds, and retained a rock-solid body.

The morning of the break-in at Janet LeGrand's house, Buck was shaving when he got the call from Henry.

"Hey Buck, we have a mission."

"Yes, sir," he answered, wiping the residual shaving cream off his face.

"I don't have time to explain. Go to Janet's and check around her property. If it's all clear, escort her to the gallery. I'll be there as soon as I can."

"On my way, sir," answered Buck.

Henry didn't have to tell Buck to bring his weapon; it never left his side since he returned from the war. He tucked the Colt 1911 into his specially designed shoulder holster to accommodate the Obsidian 45 silencer.

Buck's presence comforted Janet. Her adrenaline rush faded in the car ride to the office. Waiting in her office, she looked at her watch and wondered what took Henry so long to get there. What seemed like hours were only minutes when Henry rushed in the door.

"God, I thought you'd never get here." she moaned as she rushed up, embracing Henry.

Henry gave her a comforting squeeze. "It's okay, Janet. You're safe now. We'll figure this out." Gently, he pulled away. "Did you bring the note?" he asked.

"Yes," reaching into her coat pocket.

"You don't know who followed you out of the garage?"

"Not a clue. I never saw that car before."

Henry turned to Buck, "Hey Buck, go down outside and check around to see If you see something suspicious."

"Yes, sir," Buck answered, heading out the door.

Henry reached out his hand, "Let me look at that note."

With a pensive look, he placed the note on her desk, "Come look at this with me. Study it and tell me if you recognize the writing."

"It's hard to tell," she answered.

"Did father keep correspondence from buyers?"

"Yes, buyers and sellers. They're in the files, but there's hundreds of files."

"Let's track it down and look in the Adrian account file and see if anything matches the writing on the note."

"I've looked everywhere for that file and can't find it," she said.

"Maybe it was misplaced in a European file, and when we look for the files, it might be in one."

"Possible," she answered. "Oh wait, I forgot to tell you something."

She picked up Marc Chagall's book off the coffee table, "I found this letter from the OSS's Office of European Affairs. Dated back in 1946, it's been on Father's desk and never opened; I opened it last night."

After reading the letter, Henry stood and looked out the window like he was calculating a mathematical equation. He turned to Janet and said, "You said the man on the phone sent a package to the New York Gallery?"

"That's what he said."

Henry looked at his watch, "What time does Mary Ann get to the office?"

"She rarely gets in before ten."

"It's 8:30 there now. Can you call her at home?"

"Yeah, I have her number."

"Call her and tell her to get to the office and see if a package has arrived from Europe."

Buck rushed into the office, "Hey Boss, there's a VW Van parked down the street with two guys in it looking this way."

"Really?" Henry answered. "Let's go talk to them."

Midway from dialing Mary Ann, Janet looked up and said, "I'm scared. Don't you think we ought to call the police?"

Heading out the door, Henry looked back, "Not yet. We might be able to figure this out before they get involved. Once they get involved, it's out of our hands and could become a big mess."

"It's already a big mess if you ask me. Don't forget someone broke into my house with me asleep in bed."

"Which leads to who might have your house key. Call Mary Ann and rack your brain about who might have a key."

"Please be careful. This could be dangerous," she said as she finished dialing.

Henry gave her a fleeting nod as he hurried to catch up with Buck.

Janet's blood pressure rose as Mary Ann's phone rang, and it switched to the answering machine.

"Oh God, not now," she screeched. Then, panicked, she spoke into the answering machine, "Mary Ann, this is Janet. Call me back as soon as you can. This is very important."

To add to her anxiety, she watched from the office window as Henry and Buck approached the van. The van pulled away from the curb as a shot rang out from inside. Buck turned, pulled out his weapon, dropped to one knee, faced the fleeing van, and unleashed five rounds, shattering the rear window. The van turned sharply around the corner and sped off.

Buck stood up and looked at Henry. "Are you ok?"

Henry checked his body, "I think so. Do you see any blood?"

"No blood," Buck answered.

They looked at the building behind them and noticed a corner brick pulverized. The spent bullet lay on the sidewalk.

Janet shook like a leaf after she watched the spectacle on the street.

When they returned to the office, Henry looked concerned Buck calmly reloaded his pistol.

Janet looked at Henry with pleading eyes. "We have to call the police," she muttered, almost crying.

Henry turned to Janet. "This is a serious situation. If these people are who I think they are, the police won't be able to help much. Did you call Mary Ann?"

"I called her, but she didn't answer. I left a message on her answering machine."

Henry looked at his watch, pondered, then asked, "What about the key? Could you think of who might have one?"

"The only person I thought of was Brian."

"Brian…the chef?" Henry asked.

"Yes," she answered.

"Do you have anything with his handwriting on it?"

"I might. We must look."

The phone rang. Janet looked at Henry and Buck, locked in fear, she hesitated to pick it up.

"Are you going to pick up the phone?" scolded Henry.

Janet picked up the phone and answered feebly, "Hello…Oh! … Mary Ann, it's you. Thank God! Look, I have something important you need to do right away. Go to the office and see if a package from Dieter Hauptmann has arrived from Europe. Open it and get back to me what's in it."

A worried look came over her face as she listened to Mary Ann. She covered the mouthpiece and looked at Henry. "It came in yesterday, and she opened it. It looks like the original *Swan* by Marc Chagall."

"This is starting to make sense," Henry said under his breath.

"What did you say?" asked Janet nervously as she hung up the phone. Lost in thought, she neglected to say goodbye to Mary Ann.

"Never mind," returned Henry. "Let's find something with Brian's handwriting on it. What would he be doing with your key, anyway?"

"We had cooking classes at my place. His houseboat was too small. Sometimes, I couldn't get there in time, and I gave him a key to get set up."

"Did he ever buy artwork from you?"

"A few pieces, not much, mainly from local artists."

"Do you remember what they were?"

"One was Cubism by Martin Radloff. I gave it to him."

"Did you keep a record of it?"

"I had to pay the artist. It would be in his file."

Going to the filing cabinets, she started to open one, stood up, thought for a second, and opened the drawer below. Rummaging through the files, she pulled one out. She rifled through pages of descriptions of Radloff's artwork and receipts and found a letter from Brian thanking her for the gift.

The letter read: *Janet, thank you so much for the painting. It's perfect to hang at the foot of my bed. You're such a peach. Love, Brian.*

Henry placed the note from the fridge next to the thank you letter. After an extended gaze, "Mm...This could be our guy."

Janet stared at the two notes. *Brian... Why would Brian do such a thing?*

"Janet, Brian might not be who you think he is or be involved at all. Either way, you had better sit down. I have something to tell you that's not pretty."

Rubbing her eyes, she tiredly said, "Let me put on a pot of coffee first?"

"I'll make it," answered Henry. "You sit on the couch."

She leaned forward with her elbows on her knees, cradled her face, and talked through her hands, "This is so crazy. First, Mom and Dad died, I had to take over the business, a weird call from a German guy, awakened at night with a note in my fridge, then people were shooting at us. Who would think of putting a note in a refrigerator and finding out it's from a friend?"

Allowing the coffee to perk, Henry rolled over the desk chair and sat facing her.

"Listen, Janet. When I worked with the Navy, supplying fighter plane parts to the Russians, I was investigated by the Navy's intelligence. It almost ruined me. I found out Dad was accused of working with the Vichy French, fencing confiscated art from the Jews."

With a stunned look, "Oh bullshit!" she yelled.

"Calm down and listen! Of course, I had nothing to do with it, and after a while, it went away, but it planted a seed in the back of my brain I couldn't shake," Henry calmly explained.

Henry got up, his back to her, and poured two cups of coffee.

"After the war, I confronted Dad about what I'd heard. He laughed it off, but I could tell something was there."

Henry continued speaking as he turned, handing Janet a cup of coffee, "When I got into the airline business, I asked a friend who worked with the OSS, now CIA, if he knew of an underground network selling confiscated artwork. He said there was a large network that sold art to finance the resettlement of escaped Nazi SS to South America that's going on today."

"Why do you think Dad was involved? I never noticed any of this. He was the most loving father I've ever known. I loved him dearly!"

"That letter from the OSS he never opened tells me he was involved, but in denial. He couldn't face the reality of his involvement; your gilded eyes hid what you didn't want to see. I saw another side to Dad."

"What do you mean by my gilded eyes!?" she demanded. "Who the fuck do you think you are, coming up with this bullshit?!"

"Think about it, Janet!" he yelled. "Do you think this would happen if there weren't something to it?"

"Oh God!" She put down her cup, cradled her face, and began to sob.

Sympathetically looking at his sister, "I'm not so sure Mom and Dad's death was an accident."

Janet fell off the couch and rolled into a fetal position, uncontrollably weeping.

Henry watched Janet cry, then reached down, put her on the couch, and handed her a coffee cup.

She took her cup weakly and asked, "Do you think these people are trying to intimidate me into continuing to broker stolen art?"

"No doubt about it. These people are ruthless. They had no qualms about killing millions of people in the war and sent six million Jews to the gas chamber. The irony is that pockets of this cult have never surrendered or admitted their guilt. They are just as emphatic in their beliefs today as they were the day they began."

"This is so horrible. It's been twenty years. Will it ever end?" Janet reflected on the war years, then looked at Henry, "What I don't understand is Brian? I can't figure out how he got involved."

"His involvement is circumstantial, knowing he has a key and the writing match. What we need to do is talk to him," Henry answered.

"I'll call him right now."

"I wouldn't do that. He'll be on guard if he's involved, not telling you the truth. Somehow, we need to confront him face to face."

"How do you plan to do that?"

Henry thought momentarily, then turned to Buck, "Buck, I want you to find Brian and tail him. When the opportunity is right, we'll move in on him."

"Sure, boss. Where do I start?"

"Why don't we go to his houseboat?" Janet asked.

"There are too many people around. This might get messy; it would be better in a neutral place."

"He's cooking for the Intercontinental right now. He gets off after midnight," Janet offered.

"What kind of car does he drive?" Henry asked.

"A blue one."

"A blue one?" Henry shot back. "You don't know what it is?"

"The only make I know of is a Cadillac because I own one."

Henry stared blankly at her and then turned to Buck. "Go there tonight before closing time and order a nice dinner. When finished. ask to compliment the chef. That way, you'll know who he is and follow him, finding out where he parks his car and what it is. Then we'll go from there."

"Sure, Boss."

Janet sat on the couch, listening to Henry's plan. She tried to finish her coffee; her hands were shaking so badly she could hardly bring the cup to her lips, thinking -- *this really can't be happening.*

Chapter 6

Buck sat alone in his silver suit and pink tie at the Intercontinental Hotel's Luce Restaurant. His back against the wall, he studied the menu while finishing a glass of water.

The waiter refilled the water glass and asked, "Are you ready to order, sir?"

"Does the house salad come with the Oyster wrapped in Salmon?"

"Yes, it does, with buttered string beans."

"Who is the chef tonight?"

"Our executive chef is Brian Williams."

"I'll try those oyster wraps," answered Buck.

"Good choice," exclaimed the waiter reaching for the menu. "Would you like wine with your meal?"

"No, thank you, but keep an eye on my water glass."

"Certainly, sir. The salad will be right out."

He drained the glass of water before the waiter brought his salad. With the main course, the waiter refreshed the water glass. Buck finished the oyster wraps and string beans without leaving a scrap.

The waiter noticed Buck's empty plate and brought a tray of desserts, "We have these desserts if you would care to choose."

"No, thank you. I want to compliment the chef if he's available.

Those oyster wraps were delicious."

"Yes, sir, I'll let him know."

Brian came out, and before he got to the table, Buck stood up and offered his hand.

They shook hands vigorously as Buck said, "Those oysters were the best. I want to give you my regards, personally."

Brian smiled broadly, "Thank you. It's a little something I cooked up a while back. I'm glad you liked them."

The other patrons of the restaurant were attentive to the conversation.

"I'll be sure to return and bring my friends," Buck answered.

"Thank you again. We'll look forward to seeing you."

Brian, a showman, returned to the kitchen and waved to the enamored guests, who smiled and waved back.

Buck laid down three twenty-dollar bills. He stepped out from the back of the table, straightened his coat, entered the lobby, and asked the maître d,' "Can you direct me to the men's room?"

"Yes, sir, pass the main desk to the right."

He walked to the men's room and checked his watch; it was 11 o'clock. That gave him time to look for blue cars.

He wandered around the garage and counted three blue cars. One was a light blue Thunderbird parked behind a concrete wall with a Reserved Parking sign above. He guessed the Thunderbird was Brian's.

At midnight, Buck struggled to stay awake, sitting behind the wheel of his car. The kitchen staff got off work and entered the parking area, chatting and laughing.

He focused on the blue Thunderbird as Brian got behind the wheel, turned the key, backed out, and disappeared through the exit gate.

Chapter 7

The next morning Buck entered Janet's office. She and Henry were scouring the place for the Adrian account file.

Henry looked up, "Buck! What did you find?"

"I met him in the restaurant and waited in the parking garage. When a group of people came out, I picked him out."

Buck looked at Janet, "He got into a blue Ford Thunderbird."

"How many people were around when he left?" Henry asked.

"By my best count, six."

"That's going to make it difficult."

"That's Okay, Boss. I have a plan."

"A plan. What's that?" Janet asked nervously. "I hope it doesn't involve any violence?"

Buck looked at Janet and then back at Henry, overlooking Janet's statement. He knew what they had to do.

"I'll go up to him in the garage and start a conversation until the coast is clear. When the other people drive off, bring up your car, and we nab him and take him somewhere for a conversation," explained Buck.

"That might work. We'll try it tonight. If it doesn't, we'll have to be patient and find another way," Henry answered.

"Patience!" Janet blurted out. "Jesus, Henry, you function like this is a Sunday picnic! Now you're going to kidnap someone and rough him up. I don't want to be a part of this, Henry! Why in the hell don't we go to the police?"

Henry held his anger without shouting back, "Listen again, Janet. These Nazis are well organized and have tentacles everywhere. We need to keep as low a profile as possible. The police are always an option, but it could be an option that gets us killed."

"What are you saying, Henry? I don't understand?"

"I'll lay it out straight, Janet. There are Nazi sympathizers in the police department, and they could be a part of this whole scheme."

"Oh God! How in the hell did this happen!" Janet questioned again.

"You can thank our father," Henry answered. "He, like everybody else, didn't give a damn during the war when they sent people to the gas chambers as long as the trains were on time."

"Don't lay this shit on me, Henry. I didn't do anything except love my father."

Henry paused, looking sympathetically at his sister, "We have to face this dilemma and try to get to the bottom."

"Count me out, Henry. I'm going to the police!"

"Janet, give me two days!"

Janet began to cry again, her face buried in her hands. "Fine," she wept. "But I'm not going home. I'm so scared."

"You can stay with Ivana and me. You can wait there while Buck and I get Brian. Hopefully, it won't get messy."

"Are you kidding? I'm going with you. If he left that note in my fridge, I want to know what he thinks he's doing."

Henry and Buck looked at each other, bewildered by Janet's sudden change of heart.

Henry told Janet, "All right, you can come but pull yourself together. All your whining and crying isn't helping. You must face reality and get in control."

Janet stood up defiantly and wiped away her tears. "I'm trying to pull myself together, Henry. I'm scared and confused. It's not easy getting a handle on it. You need to be more tolerant. Last night, someone broke into my house. You were in a gunfight, and now Brian might be involved. I've had every right to be upset."

After a brief standoff, she turned away from Henry and opened another file cabinet. "If I can find that file, I'm sure it will answer many questions."

Chapter 8

Close to midnight, Henry and Janet lay low in Henry's car at the hotel parking garage. Buck stood in the shadows and waited for the kitchen staff to come out.

The kitchen service door opened as the staff entered the parking area. Brian was not with them.

"Where is he?" muttered Janet under her breath.

"Patience," whispered Henry.

Buck stood in the shadows as the kitchen staff got in their cars and drove off.

The service door opened again, and Brian walked out. He stood by his car door and fitted the key into the lock as Buck strolled by. Brian turned his head. Henry started his car.

"Mr. Williams, nice to see you again."

Brian jumped. Startled, he looked at Buck with a slight smile and said, "Oh, it's you."

Henry pulled up behind the Thunderbird to block his escape. Buck pulled out his weapon and grabbed Brian by the arm.

"What the hell?" Brian screamed out.

Janet opened the driver's side rear door as Buck shoved Brian in and forced him to the middle. Buck sat beside him and closed the door as Henry left the exit.

Brian, surprised to see Janet, "Janet, what the fuck are you doing?"

"That's what we're about to ask you?"

After a brief silence, Brian asked, "Where are you taking me?"

"To my office," answered Janet.

Brian glanced up at Buck's smiling face, then looked straight ahead.

It was an awkward drive to the office as nobody spoke. Once there, Janet rushed out to unlock the front door. Buck pulled Brian from the back seat, and he and Henry led him up the stairs.

Janet turned on the lights as Buck and Henry forced their hostage onto the couch.

Janet looked at Brian and asked, "Can I get you a drink?"

Disoriented by the offer, he nodded, "Gin and tonic?"

"I have gin and tonic, but no lime."

"That's fine. You can skip the tonic," he answered.

Janet poured a healthy amount of gin into a glass tumbler.

"We all know why we're here, don't we, Brian?"

Brian took the glass, "You tell me?" Then he took a long drink from his gin.

Janet picked up the two notes from her desk, "Do these look familiar?"

Brian gulped down the rest of his drink and held up his glass, "I need another."

She poured the second drink, "What the hell is going on, Brian? Why are you doing this?"

"I don't think you want to know."

She held the second drink in front of him, "I think I do want to know. I find myself fencing Nazi stolen art, death threats, getting shot at, and suddenly, you're in the middle of it. I want to know why."

Buck stared at Brian, took his weapon from his shoulder holster, and placed it on the counter. His hand rested over the pistol.

Brian watched Buck out of the corner of his eye and sipped his fresh drink. "It's a long story," he said.

"We've got time. We aren't going anywhere," she answered.

"Before I start, do you know who you're dealing with?"

Henry spoke for the first time, "That's what we want to know from you."

"First, let me apologize to you. I had no intention of ever getting into anything like this."

"How in the hell did you get into it?" demanded Janet.

"I'm getting to that," as he tapped his glass for another drink.

Janet obliged.

"You do realize our lives are in danger?" stated Brian.

"We realize that," answered Janet, handing him his third drink. "So go on, how did you get involved?"

"My dad," pausing to take a drink. "My dad was a Nazi sympathizer before the war. That's when he joined the Bund."

"Your dad was a member of the German American Bund, the American Nazi Party?" Henry butted in.

"That's right. He knew Fritz Kuhn when the Bund was established in Buffalo, New York. He went to Germany with Fritz and met Hitler in the early days of the National Socialist German Workers Party."

"Great stuff," injected Janet, visibly irritated. "Get down to how your father got you involved."

"That goes back to your father and a guy named Alfred Rosenburg," said Brian as he looked at Janet. "He was the Nazi Party artistic commissar, in charge of looted artwork from occupied countries. Your father became a kingpin to the operation by his buyer connections, and he and Rosenberg were on a first-name basis."

"How did you know this?" asked Janet.

"What do you think?"

"I'm having a hard time believing any of it, but go on."

"Your father was a mule for Rosenberg, selling stolen art through the

Vichy French and then later through the Nazis. These guys were making money, and we're talking about hundreds of millions. They wanted me in the loop because I knew you and your father."

"To be a spy," stated Henry.

"Yes, to be a spy."

"And you agreed?" Janet asked.

"I had no choice."

"Sounds weak, if you ask me," continued Janet.

"Look, Janet, you can abuse me all you want, but at the time, the Nazis were winning the war, and it didn't look like anything could stop them. There was a large contingent of American Nazis rooting for them. Unfortunately, my father was one of them."

"So, you went along with it." Janet chided.

"You mean like your father went along with it!" Brian yelled.

"Let's try and hold our emotions in check," warned Henry.

"If I can finish my story," said Brian, glaring at Janet.

Janet poured herself a shot of whiskey, threw her head back, and downed it, "Sure, go ahead."

"My dad's God was the Nazi party even before my family. This pipeline of stolen art was making lots of money. Besides the Jews, the Nazis were roasting homosexuals. When my father learned I was queer, he gave me two choices, work for him or die. I didn't want to die; I didn't have the stomach for it."

"You never thought about going to the authorities?" she asked.

"Are you kidding me? That would be a death sentence!"

After a pause, Brian continued, "Now I have a message for you. Your parents' death wasn't an accident."

"By what you've told us, that seems apparent," injected Henry.

"Your father wanted out. He knew the CIA was getting close to figuring out who he was. The new Nazi Wehrmacht operating in South America wanted him out of the way, figuring it would be easier to deal with you. You are a woman. Besides, you weren't a suspect."

"Well! They're fucking nuts, there's no way in hell I'm going to deal with them!" blustered Janet.

"That's what they thought you'd say. They left a package for you in the Adrian account file."

"I've looked everywhere for that file. I don't think it exists," said Janet.

"Did you look under the couch I'm sitting on?"

Flustered, Janet asked, "Do these people know you're here?"

"They are just down the street."

"You never thought about telling me this?"

"They have their ways; I just take orders. They planned to have me be the go-between. Now that you kidnapped me, it will work out better for them. It's something they can hold over your head."

Janet snapped her head around and glared at Henry. Henry looked at Buck, knelt, searched under the couch, and pulled out the file.

Henry placed the file on the desk and opened the folder. Inside were photos of Janet with people at different galas she attended with her father. They were smiling big and holding up drinks, and artwork was on the wall behind them.

He and Janet flipped through the photos while Brian informed them, "Those people in the photos standing next to you are known Nazi operatives. The Nazis that confiscated Jewish artwork."

Next were photos of receipts worth hundreds of thousands of dollars.

"You will notice your signature on those receipts of the stolen artwork, Janet," Brian finished.

"I had no idea!" shouted Janet.

"That might be true, but you'll have difficulty explaining that to the authorities."

"You son of a bitch!"

"I am a son of a bitch, Janet, but it's kept me alive!"

Brian went to the desk, picked up a pen, and wrote on a tablet.

Your office is bugged, and I want to collaborate with you. Play along until we can talk.

Henry read the note and whispered in Buck's ear. Henry searched under the furniture as Buck looked in the high places, behind pictures, anywhere that could hide a hearing device.

As they searched, Brian kept talking, "So you see, Janet, you have no choice but to go along and keep the operation going."

Janet poured herself another whiskey, sat behind her desk, downed her drink, and stared deeply into Brian's eyes, "I guess you're right. We don't want anything horrible to happen to you, do we?" She squinted her eyes, pressed her lips together, and then gave him the middle finger.

Buck found the listening device under the windowsill that looked down on the street.

"I guess there's nothing else to discuss," said Janet. "Buck, use my car and take this piece of shit back to his car."

Buck reached down and pulled Brian up by the armpit.

"One more thing, I'll be your point of contact. Conduct your business as usual," Brian instructed.

"Get him the fuck out of here!" shouted Janet.

Chapter 9

L efty walked up to Tony's desk, rolled up the morning paper and slapped it three times on his desk.

"Hey Tone, the police report in the paper stated some girls saw Brian Williams get roughed up and thrown in a car at the Intercontinental," quoted Lefty.

"When did that happen?" I asked.

"Night before last. The paper said police officers went to his houseboat to check on him, and no one was there, but the next night, he was at the hotel working."

"That's strange. Did the article say what happened?"

"The cops questioned him, and he told them he didn't know what they were talking about."

"Crazy stuff happens in that part of town," I answered. "Hey Jim, could you bring me another drink?"

"Coming right up," answered the bartender. "How about you, Lefty? Are you ready for another one?"

Lefty finished his bottle, "Sure." He asked me, "When did you last see Brian?"

"It's been a while. I haven't had much to do with him since I left the houseboat and moved to the Great Highway in Ocean Beach."

"What about Janet? Didn't you spend time together?"

"We went our separate ways after Whiskey died. We're not on good terms."

"I remember… Still weird about Brian," answered Lefty, gulping the last of his Coors. "I have to take off. I have a date tonight."

"I do too, but I'll hang out for a bit more."

Lefty got off his stool and started walking to the door.

"Hey, Lefty, didn't you forget something?" I shouted.

Turning to me, "What? Oh yes, I'm short on cash. I'll pick it up next Thursday."

Shaking my head, I sipped my Jack Daniels on the rocks.

Chapter 10

Francois Meyer got off his flight from Paris to New York City, at the same time, Brian Williams was muscled up the stairs to Janet's office. He came to retrieve what was his. Through Jewish underground networking, he knew where to find it.

As the Milice police arrested his parents back in the year 1943, young Francois ran out of the secret exit his father made down Ave. Des Roches to the harbor. His Uncle Mordecai's small commercial fishing boat lay stern to, tied to the sea wall. Francois's hair and face were soaking wet as water beads dripped off his woolen coat from the misty rain. He wiggled under the cockpit cover and lay there until his uncle arrived to go out to the fishing grounds before the first light. This plan was conceived well in advance.

He didn't wait long until footsteps were heard on the seawall, and the boat rocked as his uncle came aboard.

Mordecai heard a whisper as he began to roll up the canvas, "Uncle Mordecai."

"Francois," he whispered back. "Go forward to the anchor locker, cover yourself up with this tarp, lay still, and stay quiet."

Francois went forward as his uncle started the engine. After Mordecai released the lines, he slowly maneuvered the boat out of the harbor.

On the open sea, "Come out now, tell me what happened."

"The Milice came and arrested my parents and took them away," said Francois, tears running down his cheeks.

"Stop crying," his uncle ordered. "You must be brave; we all must be brave. Have you anything to eat?"

Shaking his head, "I don't have anything."

Mordecai opened a duffel bag and broke off a piece of bread, "You have your warm coat, and your mother left clothes for you on the boat."

He cut a hunk of cheese and handed it to the boy. He watched him eat and opened a bottle of red wine; he had a drink and then gave it to Francois. "Drink this," he commanded.

Mordecai wasn't going to do any fishing today. It would take all day to motor down the coast to Fos-sur-Mer to meet Rabbi Leo Cohen, leader of the Jewish underground. Francois would go to a safe house with other Jewish children to await a clandestine hike over the Pyrenees into Spain, then neutral Portugal.

August 25th, 1944, France was liberated from the Third Reich; Francois reunited with his uncle, who survived the occupation and reclaimed his family home, minus the family treasures. Francois lived with his uncle until he came of age. He returned to the house on Ave. Des Roches and joined the Communist Party determined to avenge the death of his parents.

During a gala at the Musee des Beaux, he met Robert and Janet LeGrand in Marseille. He secretly searched for his stolen treasure.

This search brought him to New York. Francois hailed a cab at LaGuardia Airport and instructed the driver to take him to the LeGrand Gallery in Greenwich Village. He paid for the cabbie and turned to the door where a sign hung. *Due to a death in the family, the Galley will close for a month to reorganize. Sorry for the inconvenience.*

Chapter 11

G ermans began migrating to Argentina in 1827. They founded Colonias Alemanas in the province of Buenos Aires. By 1932, more than 72,000 Germans had integrated into the Argentine cities and countryside.

The Patagonia Region, adjacent to the Andes Mountains, favored the Swiss Alps. German descendants established the Ski Resort of San Carlos de Bariloche on the shores of the glacial lake Nahuel Huapi.

Bariloche resembled a European Alpine village with Germanic chocolate stores and beer parlors lining the well-kept streets.

Argentina's large population of Germans, Spanish, and Italians sided with the Axis powers during the Second World War. The reward was billions of dollars in stolen Nazi booty transferred via German U-boats to Argentine banks.

Late in the war, Martin Bormann, the personal secretary to Adolf Hitler, recognized the war was lost and set up a network with the Catholic Church and Spanish and Argentine governments to smuggle Nazi leadership out of Europe to the safety of South America. He hoped to establish a Fourth Reich in Latin America. To accomplish his goal, he needed the Inspiration of Adolf Hitler.

While Russians closed in on the Reich Chancellery, Martin Bormann whisked Adolf Hitler, his dog Blondi, and Eva Braun from the Fuhrer bunker through underground tunnels to a secret airfield. They flew to Denmark, where a larger plane flew them to Spain, then to the Canary Islands. There, Hitler, Blondi, and Eva Braun boarded submarine U-518, captained by Hans Offerman, for an underwater trip to the deserted beach Nacoochee on the coast of Argentina. Once on shore, they enjoyed the hospitality of faithful collaborators until they arrived at their secluded home, Inalco, on the shore of Lake Nahuel Huapi, sixty miles south of San Carlos de Bariloche.

Chapter 12

Henry picked up the ringing phone. "Henry!" shouted Janet. "This girl on a bicycle delivered a note from Brian. He wants to meet us at one o'clock on Saturday afternoon at the yacht club in Inverness on Tomales Bay. Says he chartered a boat."

"Doesn't sound like a pleasure cruise," answered Henry.

"It doesn't. He wants to escape from listening ears and be out of sight."

"I'll pick up Buck and meet you at Fisherman's Wharf. Your pink Cadillac might be a bit conspicuous."

Low overcast blocked the sun as a light breeze blew over the surface of Tomales Bay. Henry, Janet, and Buck put on light coats as the three walked from the parking lot to Inverness Yacht Club. Brian waited for them on the floating dock. An 18-foot open runabout with a twenty-five horse Scott Atwater outboard, was tied off at the ready. A wicker basket lay under the foredeck. No handshakes greeted Brian as they stood looking at each other.

"I'm not sure we'll have enough room for four of us," said Brian.

"Considering the people you run with, we're going to have to make room," countered Janet.

"Okay," shrugged Brian. "Mr. Buchanan, you and Henry take the midship bench and Janet back with me. Hopefully, that will balance us out."

Settled in the boat, Brian started the Scott Atwater, let go of the lines, and put the motor in gear. Clear of the marina traffic, he opened the throttle and sped through the light chop to the middle of the bay.

After ten minutes of hard running, he cut the engine and dropped the anchor in twenty feet of water. He then picked up the wicker basket, sat down, and placed it on his lap.

Opening the basket, "Again, I want to apologize for this horrible mess. I know there is no way to make up for it except to explain it as best I can."

Buck took out the pistol from his shoulder holster. He didn't know what Brian had in the basket.

Startled, he said, "Oh, I'm sorry, Mr. Buchanan. I thought it would be nice to have some refreshments while we talked," showing him the contents. "Would you care for a glass of wine?"

"No, thank you, never touch the stuff. I only drink water."

"Oh dear," answered Brian. "I neglected to bring water."

Buck nodded his head.

"How about you, Janet, and Henry? I brought white and red wine, cheese, and salami."

Janet didn't speak as Brian opened the wine. Pouring a half wineglass, he handed it to Janet. She took the glass and placed it on her lips for a taste.

As he poured Henry a glass, "Here it is briefly. One thing the Allies, Nazis, the Vatican, and Juan Peron of Argentina had in common was fear and hatred for Joseph Stalin and Communism."

He continued as he cut slices of salami and cheese. "They were afraid the Russians would keep marching on, and the West didn't want Russia to have the Nazi advanced technology. If it came to blows, they wanted the trained German Wehrmacht to help fight them off."

"As in rocketry and the atom bomb the Nazis were developing," added Henry,

Brian offered Buck the plate of salami and cheese, "That's right, plus various other advances and millions in artwork and bullion. Martin Bormann cut a deal with the West through emissaries called Operation

Paperclip. If the West would turn a blind eye toward Hitler, he would ensure they'd get the best of the technological advances. The art and bullion were another matter. They saved that to establish the Fourth Reich."

Buck took three pieces of cheese and salami, and Henry did too. Janet waved him off, but touched her glass for a refill.

Brian continued as he poured the wine for Janet, "While Roosevelt was alive, it was an impossible offer. He didn't want to betray Stalin. After he died, I don't know the details of what went down, but from very reliable resources, Hitler and Eva Braun escaped to Argentina."

Janet finally spoke, "Why would Argentina be so stupid?"

"Because Juan and Evita Peron were fascists, and they supported the Axis powers who were dumping billions of stolen wealth in trade for sanctuary for the Third Reich. Martin Bormann wanted to start the Fourth Reich and needed Hitler as the inspirational leader."

"That's all great, Brian, but what's this stuff got to do with us?" pushed Janet.

"I'm getting to that," answered Brian, topping off her glass.

"They moved Adolf and Eva to a heavily secured mansion sixty miles south of San Carlos de Bariloche on Lake Nahuel Huapi. The only way in was by boat or seaplane, heavily guarded by former Nazi troops. At first, it was idyllic for Hitler and Eva. Hitler and Eva's daughter, Ursula, joined them from Europe. Before long, Eva was tired of confinement. Wanting her daughter to experience the wonders of life, she separated from Hitler and moved to a small village. The organization continued to look after them."

"I'm getting tired, Brian. Would you please get to the point? I'm not sure I believe any of this bullshit," shouted Janet.

"Janet! You need to know this. What I will tell you will be your only hope of survival!"

"More wine, please," was her response.

"Way before this," Brian continued. "Back in the 1930s, not sure of the date, your father was at a gala with Adolf and Eva. Your Father was a heartthrob of women. Unfortunately, Eva Braun was one of them. At the time, she felt hurt that Hitler was neglecting her. She and your father had an encounter."

As Brian said this, Janet took a drink of her wine. In shock, she spit her wine all over Brian, "Shut the fuck up, Brian, you're making me sick."

Brian reached for a towel and wiped the wine from his face. "Janet!" he yelled. "You have to listen to me."

"So, what are you saying?" she yelled back.

'I'm saying, Janet, you are the illegitimate daughter of Eva Braun. You've got to contact her and tell the organization to back off. They still listen to her."

"Oh my God. How can this be true?" Janet responded. "How did I get chosen to be in such a fucked-up situation?"

"I guess you were born in the wrong place at the wrong time," answered Brian.

The boat went quiet. Brian placed the wine bottle in the wicker basket and put it back under the foredeck. He pulled the anchor, started the motor, and headed for the dock.

Standing on the dock, Janet asked, "How do I find her?"

"I don't know. That's for you to figure out. You can start by looking in Bariloche," answered Brian.

Chapter 13

Rain poured outside Tony Nik's as Lefty and I sat comfortably nursing drinks on a gray, dark Thursday.

"Big news in the paper last night," said Lefty, slowly tearing the wet label off his bottle of Coors.

I took a drink of my Jack Daniels, a drag of my Camel, and exhaled through my nose and mouth and took the bait. "What was that?"

"They found Brian Williams dead on Francis Drake Boulevard out at Tomales Bay."

I turned my head, looked directly at Lefty, "You gotta be shitting me!"

"No, I'm not. His car smashed against a redwood tree. They thought the crash killed him until they found a bullet in his brain."

After a long pause, "Probably had something to do with that incident at the hotel," I answered.

"Probably so," said Lefty while he gathered the wet label pieces and put them in the ashtray. "I wonder what kind of weird shit he was into. You think that Janet chick might have something to do with it?"

"It wouldn't surprise me. She spent time with Andy Warhol types. Plus, her brother has major government connections. I'll tell you this, after what she's gotten me into, I'm staying far away from anything she's got going!"

"Don't blame you," answered Lefty. "We got enough shit going on here to last a lifetime."

"Got that right," draining my glass of Jack Daniels.

Chapter 14

Janet lay in bed for the third straight day, unable to cope, trying to absorb what she heard about what happened on Tomales Bay. When she heard Brian was dead, she feared what might come next. With no energy to move, her coping mechanism no longer functioned. She couldn't conform to normal life.

Hearing a voice, "Who is it?" she yelled.

"Your brother. Where are you?"

"I'm in bed." she weakly shouted.

Slowly Henry opened her bedroom door, "What are you doing? I've been calling you all day."

"I can't answer the phone, Henry. I can't deal with this."

"Janet! Get up! This is not the time to fall apart!"

"You don't understand! My life was so beautiful… now this happens."

"Your life was beautiful, but it was a charade. You were blind to what fueled your happiness."

"Do you have to be so cruel? Can't you see what misery I'm in?"

Henry stared at her. She stared back, fear and anguish in her eyes.

"When was the last time you ate?"

"I can't eat, Henry."

He reached down and pulled her out of bed, "Come on. I'm going to make you some bacon and eggs."

Weakly standing, she asked, "Do you have any Diazepam?"

Chapter 15

Francois checked into his hotel on West 8th Street. Pulling a card out of his pocket, he checked the number and dialed LeGrand Gallery, New York. On the tenth ring, with no answer, he reluctantly hung up.

He called the front desk. "Reception," they answered.

In his strong French accent, "This is Francois Meyer in room 221; I need to make a long-distance phone call to San Francisco. Is that possible?"

"Dial 9 before you dial, and the call will be billed to your room."

"Merci beaucoup," he answered and hung up.

He dialed the LeGrand Gallery in San Francisco with the same results, but there was no answer.

Frustrated, he called the front desk again, "Reception."

"Could you inform me where the nearest Western Union office is?"

"Four blocks from here at West 4th and Broadway."

His frustration increased as he hung up. He then sat at his desk and wrote a letter on hotel stationery.

Dear Mr. LeGrand or to whom this may concern,

I am Francois Meyer. We met at the Musee des Beaux-Arts in Marseille. I am searching for the painting The Swan by Marc

Chagall, which Vichy stole from my family in 1943. I understand from reliable sources that the LeGrand Gallery should be or shortly will be in possession of my property.

I desire to resolve this civilly before I take more desperate measures to redeem my property.

My contact is at the Marlton Hotel, 5 West 8th St, NY, NY, Phone, 212 555 8273.

Francois Meyer

He walked to the Western Union office to have it delivered to both galleries.

Chapter 16

Three hours later…Janet took a Valium and finished her breakfast; Henry coaxed her to shower. While he was washing the breakfast dishes, the phone rang.

Going toward the bathroom, he yelled over the sound of the water, "The phone's ringing; you want me to answer it?"

"Oh God, I don't want to talk to anybody!"

Henry ignored her and picked up the phone, "Janet LeGrand residence," he answered.

"This is Jennifer at the gallery. Is Miss LeGrand home?"

"She's in the shower. Can I have her call you back?"

Jennifer needed an answer. The delivery man was waiting: "There is a Western Union deliveryman here with a telegram from Francois Meyer for her father. I don't know if I should sign for it."

"Jennifer, this is Henry, Janet's brother. Sign for it, and we'll be down there as soon as possible."

"Yes, Mr. LeGrand, I'll sign and place it on her desk."

"That's good, Jennifer. Thank you."

Janet walked in with a towel around her middle and one gathered on her head.

"Who was that?" she asked.

"Jennifer at the gallery. A telegraph came to the gallery from Francois Meyer, and she wanted to know if she should sign for it."

"Francois Meyer! Oh God, what does he want?"

"Do you know him?" asked Henry.

"Yes, I know him. Father and I met him at a gala in Marseille, and I've run into him a few times since. He told us his parents died at Auschwitz concentration camp. He was looking for a picture stolen from his family by the Vichy French."

"As hard as this might be for you, it might be another puzzle piece. Do you know anything else about him?" asked Henry.

"From mutual friends, I heard on the QT that he's linked to an underground communist Jewish group. They are hunting down escaped Nazis who killed their families. There is no joy in the guy. He never smiles, always wears black, and I heard he's gay."

Henry pondered her words silently.

Janet continued, "I'm trying to figure out what you mean by another puzzle piece. First, we have Nazis demanding we keep selling stolen art, or they are going to kill us. Now we have communist Jews who want their stuff back, and if they don't get it, they'll kill us. And you don't want to go to the police."

Henry disregarded Janet's last statement, "Get dressed. We must go to the gallery and find out what Francois wants."

"Damn you, Henry!" Janet shouted and stormed off to her bedroom.

Chapter 17

J anet read the telegram at the office, "What do you think he means by more desperate measures?"

"I don't know for sure; I don't think he'll go to the police."

"Why not?"

"This organization operates clandestinely, not within the norms of international law."

"Damn it, Henry! Here you go again. Please tell me why they'd do such a thing?"

"After what the Jews have been through, they don't trust anybody. Israel is a Jewish state surrounded by enemies, all of which want them annihilated. Desperate measures could mean anything. Francois wants his artwork back, and it's in your office in New York. Are you going to give it to him?"

In a huff, Janet picked up the phone and called the New York office.

"Who are you calling?" asked Henry.

Janet raised her hand at Henry as Mary Ann picked up the phone. "Mary Ann, Janet, I want you to get *The Swan* by Marc Chagall out of the office. If anybody asks, tell them we don't have it; we never had it. Do you understand?"

"Okay," answered Mary Ann. "What do you want me to do with it?"

Janet put her hand over the phone and looked at Henry, "She wants to know what to do with it?"

"We should have talked about this first!" Henry blasted out.

"I'm sick of talking about it! Now what should she do with it?"

"Tell her to take it to Pennsylvania Station and put it in a large locker. Put the key in an accessible place where we can reach it, then take two weeks off, go to the Bahamas, and don't come back until we call her."

"Why all that?" asked Janet.

"Just do it, God damn it! Tell her I'll arrange everything and send the itinerary by telex. I'll tell you after she hangs up."

After Mary Ann had been given the message, Janet hung up and looked at Henry. "Okay, why the Bahamas?"

"You just put her life in jeopardy. We are the only people who know where the painting is. We must make sure nobody gets to her."

"I didn't think of that," answered Janet.

"That's why we should have talked about it, but getting it out of the office is clever. Now what are you going to tell the Frenchman?"

"I'm not going to tell him anything. He doesn't know I've read the telegram."

"He knows somebody signed for it." Henry pondered briefly. "Maybe we can get him to work in our favor."

"How's that?" asked Janet.

"I'm not sure yet."

Chapter 18

Francois hadn't anticipated waiting to check on his property until the Gallery reopened. There would be people working inside to reorganize the gallery. Somehow, he had to make contact. He hoped the telegram would open a door. The value of the painting justified his search for help. Before he'd left Europe, he received the phone number of Robert Gorman, the leader of the Jewish underground network in New York City. Now was the time to reach out to him.

Robert Gorman picked up the ringing phone, "Hello."

"My name is Francois Meyer; I'm visiting New York from France, and I received your number from Rabbi Leo Cohen."

"I know Rabbi Cohen very well. He's been here many times. How can I help you."

"I'm here to recover my stolen property from the war, and I've run into a snag. The Rabbi told me to reach out to you if I had problems. To be honest, I don't like discussing issues over the phone. Would it be possible to meet somewhere?"

"I'm in Brooklyn. We can meet for lunch at Junior's Cheesecake tomorrow at noon."

"Thank you very much, Mr. Gorman; I'll take a cab and meet you at noon."

"Francois… call me Bob. You had better get there by 11:30. It gets crowded at noon."

"I'll be there. Au revoir."

Chapter 19

Mary Ann couldn't sleep. She wondered what to take to the Bahamas on such short notice. Something about that painting made her anxious.

She gave up trying to sleep and packed the best she could, not neglecting her three two-piece bathing suits.

She dozed off and was aroused by the alarm set for five. After a quick cup of coffee, she dressed and lifted a large empty suitcase to walk three blocks from her residential flat to the gallery.

Francois was up early, walking toward the gallery, smoking a cigarette. Mary Ann opened the front door carrying a large suitcase.

He quickened his step and checked the front door. It was locked. He sat down on a bus stop bench across the street and lit a cigarette to wait.

Mary Ann put down the suitcase, went to the Model 33 teletype machine, and ripped off the message from Henry.

Mary Ann. After you deliver the painting to Penn Station, drop the key in an addressed envelope and send it to the office in San Francisco. You are booked for the 2 pm Eastern Airline flight 657 to Miami, then flight 37 with Bahama Airlines on their seaplane to Nassau, Bahamas. You have reservations at the Graycliff Hotel on West Hill Street. Take one thousand dollars from the petty cash drawer in the safe for your needs. When you get there, open a bank account where we can transfer funds as needed.

Have a great flight, Henry.

PS Burn this message once complete.

The Swan, still in its protected crate, fit perfectly in the suitcase. Mary Ann closed the case and locked it. She put the key on a sting that fit comfortably in the cleavage between her 36 D breasts. She placed the thousand dollars in an envelope and tucked it beneath the Elastic band in her underpants.

She wrote down the flight instructions and hotel address, lit a match, and burned the message in an ashtray on the desk. On another envelope, she wrote down the gallery address in San Francisco and placed a stamp in the upper right-hand corner.

Ready to leave, she realized she'd be carrying a painting worth over $100,000 and $1,000 cash tucked into her panties back to her flat. She figured nobody would be on the streets. Still, she checked and looked out the office window.

She saw a tall man dressed in black sitting at the bus stop smoking a cigarette. He glanced up, and their eyes met and lingered for a second.

She turned away and checked her watch. The 6:02 bus would arrive shortly. She sat down in the office chair and waited. When the bus arrived, she looked out the window, hoping the man had disappeared. The bus pulled away. The man in black looked up, and their eyes met again.

Mary Ann picked up the phone and dialed.

"Yellow cab."

"I need a pick-up right in front of LeGrand Gallery."

"Yes, ma'am, 10 minutes."

"Please ensure the driver parks right in front of the door."

'Will do, ma'am."

She worked her way to the front door, hoping not to be seen. The cab arrived and honked the horn. Hurriedly, she exited and set down the case as she locked the door. Francois rushed up to her with her hand on the cab's rear door.

"Do you work here?" he excitedly asked.

She pushed the case inside the back seat, "I'm the cleaning lady."

"Please, I need your help," begged Francois.

Caught off guard, she looked up at him.

"I need to talk with Robert LeGrand. It's very important."

She slid in the back seat and focused straight ahead, "Robert LeGrand is dead." she screamed.

"Dead," he jerked. "Who's the owner now?"

"You have to wait until they re-open," closing the cab door.

"Drive on," she said to the driver.

Their eyes met again as the cab drove off. Francois didn't know his family treasure slipped from his grasp less than a foot away.

Chapter 20

At 10:30 am, Francois paid the cab driver and stood before Junior's Restaurant and Bakery, not knowing what Bob Gorman looked like.

A 30ish, slim, well-dressed man in a tailored suit carrying a small briefcase and walked up to him, "Francois?"

"Bob Gorman?" queried Francois.

Shaking hands, Bob opened the door and gestured for Francois to enter. As they passed a glass case full of different cheesecakes, Bob pointed to an empty table in the corner.

Sitting down, "This place is famous for its cheesecakes," explained Bob.

Francois didn't smile as the waitress came to the table, poured water into their glasses, and handed them menus.

Looking at the menu, "What do you suggest?"

"I always get the corn beef sandwich," answered Bob.

Briefly, Francois studied the menu. "I'll have the same."

Before the waitress returned, "How was your fight across the pond?" asked Bob.

"My flight was fine," answered Francois rudely. "But I have more important things to discuss."

Pausing to give the waitress their order, Bob, unshaken by Francois's rudeness, answered, "Yes, we're aware of that."

Bob took a drink from his water. "We are aware of your situation. Rabbi Cohen told us your stolen property would be coming to New York. We know your history and that you are a French Communist."

"You heard this from the Rabbi?"

"We know you plan to go to South America and seek the Vichy police officer who sent your parents to the concentration camp and have him brought to justice."

"And he told you this?"

"We know you planned to get back your valuables and sell them to finance your venture."

Francois took a drink from his water, "Go on."

"Our cell of the Jewish underground motto is *Never Again*. We're not in good stead with some Jewish groups because we mean what we say. We're considered a terrorist organization. We'll go to any length to defend Jews. We'll help you, but you must understand we've done much groundwork, and you can't barge your way around disrupting operations," said Robert.

The waitress brought the sandwiches, giving Francois time to reflect on what he had heard.

Gorman took a bite of his sandwich, then continued, "We've known for some time that Robert LeGrand was working with the Nazis, selling stolen art to finance their operations in South America. Robert's death wasn't an accident. We fed the Nazis and Robert bogus information that made them begin to distrust each other. The Nazis wanted Robert out of the way and had him and his wife killed."

"They're pretty good at that," stated Francois, chewing the last of his sandwich. "Do you know who's going to take over the galleries?"

"We assume it will be Janet, their daughter."

"I met Janet and her father in Marseille. What I didn't know was that her father was dead, and the gallery closed for a month. I tried to call but didn't get an answer, so I sent a telegram."

"If she didn't know, she would know by now of her father's activities with what they call the Adrian account. I doubt she'll talk to you. If she does, the Adrian account will be your buzzword.

"What's the Adrian account?" asked Francois.

"That's the file for Robert LeGrand's transactions with the Nazis. It was too risky to sell hot items to ignorant buyers because they could blow the whistle on the operation once they figured it out. There are buyers who know the rules and are willing to buy the merchandise."

Francois soaked in this added information and realized he wasn't alone. A crack appeared in his hard shell as he warmed up to Bob Gorman and the organization he represented.

He felt he was among friends in whom he could confide his frustrations: "I feel stuck here in New York. I can't hang around here forever."

"The way I see it, you have two options. You can wait until the gallery reopens or go out and try to catch Janet in San Francisco. Do you know someone who might know how to find her?"

"Actually, I do, a guy named Tony Taylor. He was in the Army in Germany. Janet brought him to an art gala in Marseille, we met there, and I ran into him in Chile. He runs an escort service."

"That's an interesting line of work. That might be your best bet. If you go down to South America to try and find this Vichy police officer, you'd better be aware of what's happening."

"What's happening?" questioned Francois.

"Former Nazis run the place. Others struck out trying to do the same thing you are and were never heard from again."

"Do you know people there?"

"We have connections, but it's not easy for a fresh Jew to arrive and start asking a bunch of questions unless you have a death wish," said Bob, waving over the waitress. "Do you have an idea where to start looking?"

Before he answered, the waitress handed Bob the bill, which came to $28. Bob placed it on the table, with $15 on top. Francois got the hint and did the same.

Francois answered as he got up from the table, "A place called San Carlos de Bariloche."

Bob stopped as he walked to the exit, took Francois by the arm, looked him square in the face, "That's only the most secure Nazi stronghold in Argentina. It's rumored that Hitler and Eva Braun are close to there on Lake Nahuel Huapi. You had better produce Plan B."

Bob Gorman pulled out his card and pen and wrote on the back. "Here, take this. The address I wrote on the back is where you can find help. Don't use it unless you absolutely must."

Francois glanced at the card and warmly held out his hand. Gorman shook it, saying, "Shalom."

Chapter 21

Janet and Henry searched their father's accounting ledger for clues when Jennifer knocked on the door jamb.

Turning to look at her, "There's this old oriental couple knocking on the front door."

"Did you direct them to the sign?" asked Janet.

"I did, but they shook their finger at me. The old lady said it was important they talk to you."

Janet looked at Henry, "What do you think?"

"Let's go talk to them. This could be another clue."

"You and your goddamn clues," said Janet, heading down the stairs with a bundle of keys in her hand.

At the front door, Janet and Henry couldn't believe what they saw.

The Asian man, in his eighties, stooped over a polished ash cane. He wore a white suit and black tie, and his fedora hat was banded black. Rimless glasses hung off the tip of his stunted nose.

The woman was years younger. She weighed ninety pounds and was not five feet tall. Her flowered pink and yellow dress came below her knees, and a wide-brimmed straw hat covered her head.

When the door opened, they both bowed, he a little further than he stooped. The lady opened the conversation.

"So sorry to bother you. I introduce Mr. Akia Ishikawa and Michiko Seco. We are here to discuss the Adrian account, very important."

Janet and Henry, stunned by their appearance, were speechless, staring at the couple.

"May we come in?" the lady asked.

"Yes, yes, please come in," answered Henry, gently touching the old man's arm and guiding him in.

Janet led them to the back of the gallery to a rest space with two couches facing each other.

The lady sat down and opened the conversation, "Mr. Ishikawa speak only Japanese, German, and Portuguese, so I translate."

Janet and Henry nodded their approval.

"So sorry about mother and father, and Brian was a good friend."

"How did you know about Brian? And he wasn't a good friend at all," snarled Janet.

Henry snapped his head toward Janet and held his hand to his lips. Janet folded her arms, leaned against the couch, and glared at the two Asians.

Mr. Ishikawa spoke so softly they could hardly hear.

"Very important, Adrian's account stays open. It is dangerous for you not to stay open," the lady translated.

He spoke again, and she translated: " Merchandise comes to galleries, selected buyers come, pay cash."

Reaching into his coat pocket, he held out an envelope.

"Banking information: São Paulo, Brazil, needs to open to transfer funds through father's special account with Lloyds Bank."

Mr. Ishikawa placed the envelope on the glass table. Henry turned to Janet. "Sao Paulo has the largest Japanese population outside of Japan."

Janet glared at her guests and prodded, "So what?"

"You take $10,000 to Sao Paulo and open an account in your name."

"Jesus, you people don't ask for much. How do you expect us to pull that off?"

Miss Seco nodded her head up and down, smiling. "You can do it. You must complete by the second of next month."

Miss Seco leaned toward Mr. Ishikawa and said, "When package come New York gallery, must process immediately."

Janet glared at the couple, "You saw on the door that we're closed for the next few weeks. Nothing is processed until we complete our transition. And as of now, we have no knowledge of any package."

Ishikawa spoke softer, and the lady translated, "So sorry, could be unfortunate for you."

"So, what are you going to do, kill us too? We're the last in the line if we go. Nothing happens on your end, so think about it. Tell your handlers we got the message and get back to us in three weeks." Janet snapped.

Janet abruptly stood up, "Henry, please show Mr. Ishikawa and Miss Seco out, I have work to do upstairs."

Chapter 22

Lefty and I sat at the bar when Francois walked in. He stood for a moment, adjusting to the dim lighting. Lefty turned in mid-sentence to check him out and realized he wasn't from the local crowd.

Lefty turned back to me, "Hey, check that tall guy wearing all black."

I looked up, "Oh shit!"

"What's wrong? You know the guy?"

"Yeah, I know the guy. That's the problem."

"What do you mean the problem?"

"Whenever he shows up, there's trouble."

"What kind of trouble?" asked Lefty.

"Here he comes. I'll tell you later."

Francois took a seat next to me.

As nonchalantly as possible, I lifted my drink, took a sip, and looked at him. "Hello, Francois, been a while."

In a strong French accent, he replied, "Oui, Mister Tony, it has been a long time."

"Hey, Jim," I shouted. "Put this man's drink on my tab."

"What would you like, sir?" Jim answered.

"Vin rouge," he answered.

Jim being a man of the world, "The house red be okay?"

"Parfait," answered Francois.

Lefty, curious, had a lock on his face, *What the fuck's going on here?*

I took another drink, looked straight ahead expressionlessly, and asked, "What brings you to San Francisco?"

Francois put his right elbow on the bar and turned toward me. "I'm looking for Janet LeGrand. She has something that belongs to me. Do you know where I can find her?"

"I haven't seen Janet in quite a while. Did you check her gallery?"

"Oui, I checked the gallery. They closed to reorganize after her father died. I was hoping you might know where she lived?"

"Did you check the phone book?"

"Oui, Mister Tony, I checked the phone book. There is no listing for Janet LeGrand."

I turned and looked at Francois, "I don't know how you found me, but it wasn't by happenstance. I'm not interested in getting involved with anything you or Janet are into. So, if you don't mind, I'd prefer you leave me out of it."

"I can make it worth your while, Mister Tony."

I finished my drink, pulled a twenty-dollar bill out of my pocket, placed it on the bar, got off the bar stool, said, "I told you, Francois, I don't want anything you or Janet have going," and headed for the door.

"See you next week," I said, passing Lefty.

Lefty and Francois stared at each other in the mirror behind the spirits. Each took a drink. Then Lefty said, "Excuse me, Mister Frenchman, you said you'd make it worth our while. How much are you talking about?"

Francois puckered his lips and shrugged his shoulders, "Let's say five hundred dollars."

"Do you have it on you?"

Francois paused to light a cigarette, took a big drag, and exhaled a cloud of smoke, "Oui."

Lefty took another drink, "I know where Janet lives."

Chapter 23

Francois stood on Bay Street, staring at the concrete steps leading up to Janet's apartment. It looked like no one was home. He didn't know Buck watched him come up the steps.

Francois rang the doorbell, but nobody answered. He rapped loudly with his closed fist, still no answer. As he checked the handle to see if the door was locked, Buck struck him over the head with a blackjack and knocked him out cold on the concrete stoop.

Francois regained consciousness with a splitting headache. He lay on the floor with his arms and feet securely tied behind his back. Buck was on the phone.

"Yes, Mr. LeGrand, a tall guy wearing black with a hawk-billed nose.

Henry looked at Janet, "Tall guy wearing black with hawk-billed nose."

"Francois," answered Janet.

Buck had tied him to the couch when Janet and Henry entered her apartment.

"He only speaks French," Buck commented, staring at their captive.

"He speaks multiple languages," snidely remarked Janet. "You can untie him."

Janet looked at Henry and said, "Okay, we got him. How do we make him work for us?"

"Tell him the truth," answered Henry.

She turned to Francois and said, "We have your painting, but we can't give it to you."

Francois rubbed the knot on his head and grimaced in pain, "Adrian account," he answered.

"So, you know?" asked Henry.

"A man from the Jewish underground told me about it in New York."

"Oh God, please! Not another terrorist organization!" cried Janet.

Henry broke in, "If you know about the Adrian account, you know the Nazis use the proceeds to finance their operations in South America."

"Oui, I know that."

"We're on the same page and must work together to crack this nut," explained Henry.

"Before you go on, Mister Henry, let me explain. I don't care about the painting; I need to sell it for the money. I know the Frenchman who arrested my parents and sent them to the gas chambers and know where he is. I need the money to find him and avenge my parents' death," explained Francois.

"Where is he?" asked Janet.

"He lives in a village in Patagonia, Argentina."

"What is the name of the village?" asked Henry.

"San Carlos de Bariloche."

Henry and Janet looked at each other.

"That's interesting; Janet and I have business in the same village. Do you have contacts down there?" asked Henry.

"Oui, we have a Jewish underground network. With me being Jewish, it's hazardous. I can connect with the network, but we need a Goy, someone expendable to lead the investigation."

"Do you have anybody in mind?" asked Henry.

"I did, but when I asked him to help me find Miss Janet's residence, he refused, saying not to bother him again."

"How did you find my apartment?" asked Janet.

"After he left, his friend offered to help me."

"Who was that?" asked Janet.

"A sloppy man named Lefty."

"Lefty!" exclaimed Janet. "Are you talking about Lefty Jackson?"

"I don't know his last name," answered Francois.

"If it were Lefty Jackson, he wouldn't give you information for free," said Janet.

"Yes, it cost me five hundred dollars."

"Wait a minute. Did you meet him at Tony Nik's?" asked Janet.

"Oui."

"Was it Tony Taylor who you first asked?"

"Oui."

"And he refused to help."

"Oui."

Janet looked at Henry, "Tony could get the job done, and he is very expendable. We must get him on board."

"How do you plan on doing that?" Francois said. "He refused to help,"

"We are in desperate times," answered Janet. "It will take desperate measures."

Chapter 24

Janet's pink Cadillac pulled up in front of my house on the Great Highway. The sun had an inch to go before it set, and the ocean was calm. Small waves lapped on the sandy beach, and I was washing dishes in the kitchen sink.

Dressed to the nines in her bright red spaghetti strap dress, no stockings, and green sandals, she neglected her bra and underwear. Her hair tossed and tousled—it was supposed to look that way. A Serapian leather purse was under her arm. Inside were three sworn statements from former women I escorted.

I turned when I heard footsteps on the wooden front porch. All I saw was red. Janet knocked on the door, not the slightest bit nervous. She knew me well.

I opened the door, not saying anything as I checked her out.

"Are you going to invite me in?" Janet asked.

I stepped aside and allowed her to enter, but neglected to greet her. I knew this was not a friendly visit. She took a minute to wander around the interior, impressed with the decor and tidiness.

"Very nice," she stated. "Everything to make a woman feel comfortable."

Familiar with her ways, I finally spoke, "Can I get you a drink?"

"Chardonnay?"

"I have Bogle."

"My favorite," she answered.

She sat down on the couch as I went to the wine rack. I opened the bottle, poured it into two glasses, and handed it to her.

"You've got something on your mind," I said, more of a statement than a question.

I sat in the stuffed chair in front of her. She crossed her legs. She wasn't wearing underwear.

"I do," taking her first drink.

I thought back to the encounter with the Frenchman.

"Francois?" I asked.

"More than that," she answered.

After a pause, "I told Francois I wasn't going to have anything to do with whatever he or you had going."

Janet took a drink and recrossed her legs from one side to the other. "You might not have any choice in the matter," she said.

"You're wrong, Janet, and if you go on like that, you can finish your drink and leave."

Janet put down her drink, opened her purse, and took out three sworn statements.

"Do you know Margie Baumgartner, Silvia Waters, and Gloria Bartelson?"

I looked at her and remained silent.

"I believe they were so-called clients of yours."

There was no reaction as I continued to stare.

"I have these signed affidavits from each one saying you raped them."

"Bullshit!" I exclaimed.

"These are legal documents; you could be in big trouble."

"You know I didn't rape anyone."

"I don't know anything but what I read in these papers. Your occupation is very questionable. You're going to have a tough time proving otherwise."

I got up, turned my back on her, and lingered briefly with my hand on the wine bottle. Then, facing her, bottle in hand, locked eye to eye, seconds ticked away as I contemplated my predicament.

Topping off her wine glass, "What's on your mind?" I asked.

She tucked her legs under her and took another drink.

I sat unmoved, eyes still locked on to hers.

"My father was selling stolen art for the Nazis. Something went haywire, and they killed him. Brian told me they wanted me to continue the operation on the threat of death. Brian, who was working for them, is now dead. They killed him because he was trying to help us. I know it sounds crazy, but he said my father had an affair with Eva Braun, and I'm her daughter."

"You're the daughter of Eva Braun?" I answered with an unbelieving slant in my eye.

"That's what Brian said."

"I thought she and Hitler died in the bunker, and they burned the bodies."

"That's the story, but there is compelling evidence they escaped to Argentina and live on a lake resembling the Swiss Alps.

Starting to feel the jaws of entrapment, I lashed out, "I can't believe you could walk in here and lay this shit on me and expect me to jump to. I don't owe you anything. Who do you think you are?"

"Oh Tony," Janet laughed sarcastically, "The choice is up to you," waving the sworn statements in the air. "You need to know I'm dead serious."

Desperately trying to control my emotions, I gulped down my wine. Taking time to get up to pour another glass, then answered, "Just for curiosity's sake, what would be my involvement?"

"You'd go down to make a bank deposit in Sao Paulo, find Eva Braun in Argentina, and tell her to have the Nazis back off her daughter. Brian said the organization still obeys her."

I placed my drink on the side table, then rubbed my face and combed my fingers through my hair.

"You know this could get me killed?"

"No more dead than Henry, me, or Francois."

Amused by this turn of events, I wanted to hear the rest of the story.

Topping off her glass, "What's Francois got to do with it?"

"He knows where the person is who arrested his parents and sent them to the gas chambers. He wants to bring him to justice. He has connections to Jewish underground networks who could get us where we need to go to find these people."

"Why don't you use them to accomplish what you need?"

"They're Jewish. He said he needs a gentile."

Sarcastically responding to what I considered a ridiculous request, "I'm the gentile, and you're going to blackmail me to get this done?"

Janet stood up from the couch, pulled out a pistol from her leather purse, and pointed it at me.

"I brought this along to prove my point. You have until tomorrow to decide, or I will go to the police."

She placed a note on the side table. "Henry rented a warehouse to meet in. Here is the address."

Backing up to the door, she took the handle. "Tomorrow night, you will meet with Henry and Francois to formulate a plan. Be there at 7 p.m."

Opening the door, "By the way, do you snow ski?"

"I do. So what?" I answered defiantly.

"This could work out very well," she said, walking down the steps.

Chapter 25

I was having difficulty processing what happened to me when the phone rang.

"Hey, Tone," said Lefty. "You know this whole thing with Janet, that Frenchman, and Brian getting whacked. I got a handle on it."

"I don't think you do," I answered.

"I do, for sure, man. Drugs, these people are into big drug deals."

"You're wrong, Lefty. You have no idea."

"Bullshit, man, put the pieces together. They travel all over the world, have money floating everywhere, whack people who get in the way. Think about it, man, drugs."

"I've got the pieces together, Lefty. It's not drugs."

"You got the pieces together? What is it?"

"I'm not sure I can tell you," I answered.

"Don't be an asshole! What are you talking about?"

"Hey, can I call you back later? I need a little space."

"Fuck no, you can't call me back later. What is going on?" demanded Lefty.

After a pause, "Okay, listen, but you have to keep your mouth shut."

"Mum's the word, you can trust me,"

"I'm not sure about that."

"Bull shit, Man, when did I ever let you down?"

"Just listen, God damn it!"

I took a deep breath, still processing Janet's demands. "Janet wants me to go to Argentina to find Eva Braun and tell her Janet is her daughter. The Nazis are making her sell stolen art, and Eva Braun is supposed to tell them to knock it off."

"Whose Eva Braun?" asked Lefty.

"What the fuck, don't you know anything about Hitler and the Nazis?"

"Sure, I do. I know we kicked the shit out of them."

I wondered if I did the right thing by telling Lefty, but continued, "Eva Braun was Hitler's mistress and is also supposed to be Janet's mother from a liaison Braun had with Janet's father."

After a brief silence, "Wow! This is heavy shit!" said Lefty, then paused a moment more. "There's got to be big money involved in this. They're going to pay you big time?"

"No money. Janet has the names of three of my clients that say I raped them. If I don't do it, I will go to jail."

Lefty began to laugh, "This is some far-out shit man!"

"What in the hell are you laughing at, you idiot!"

Still laughing, "You must do this shit and not get paid. That's what I'm laughing at."

"Fuck you, Lefty. She laid this on me less than an hour ago. I don't know what I will do. I'll talk to you later."

"Wait, wait, don't hang up. What's next?"

"I'm to meet with them tomorrow. Look, man, I got to go," hanging up the phone.

The phone rang again; I hesitated to pick it up.

"What?"

"I'll go with you."

"You want to get involved in this shit?" I gasped.

"Hell, yes! I know there is big money in there somewhere."

"Fuck, Lefty, I'll pick you up at six.

Chapter 26

At 7 p.m., I drove up and checked the address on Janet's note. Still confused about how this was happening, I was glad Lefty wanted to come along. I hadn't decided what action to take, but I felt compelled to attend the meeting.

I parked on the street. We checked the side door and found it unlocked. Two people's voices echoed as we walked toward the middle of this huge warehouse.

Henry and Buck stood up. Henry offered his hand. I refused the offer.

I looked at Buck, "Who are you?"

"The question is, who is your friend?" Buck returned.

"I'm Lefty Jackson, Tony and I work together."

"That wasn't in the plan," answered Buck.

Henry said, "That's okay, Buck," looking at us. "This is Mr. Buchanan; he works for us as head of security."

"You know what you're doing is criminal, Mr. Buchanan?" I sarcastically stated.

Buck didn't answer, but smiled.

Janet and Francois entered the warehouse.

I sat down, facing the approaching couple. Without greetings, I investigated Janet and Francois's eyes.

Once settled, Henry proceeded, "As it stands, our lives are in danger. We face the aftermath of a worldwide conflict and the reshuffling of the world order, the defeated and victors alike."

"Let's cut through the crap!" interrupted Lefty. "We know what happened, and we know you want us to go look for some chick named Eva Braun in South America."

"Wait a moment, young man, nobody invited you here," commanded Buck.

"Listen, Bucky, get this straight, Tone, don't go anywhere without me. We'll find this chick, but it will cost you money. I mean money, big time. Otherwise, you can send Tony off to jail for raping three whores he never did. I know those sluts, and I can produce a rap sheet as long as your arm for the three of them. So, produce a number so we can go to work."

The warehouse went silent; the four accusers looked back and forth at each other, not knowing where to go from there.

I looked at Lefty. Henry looked at me, "Are you two in agreement?"

After a long silence, I looked again at Lefty and snarled, "Yeah, we're in agreement."

"Okay, we have three weeks to complete this project. Some risk might be involved," instructed Henry.

Chapter 27

Lefty and I sat at Tony Nik's while we waited for fake passports. They changed my last name to LeGrand so I could be a member of the family to open an account in Sao Paulo.

Peeling his label off the bottle of Coors, "You think that French Jew can come up with what he promised?" asked Lefty.

"I don't know, you got us into this," I snapped.

"Pretty spooky going into South America with false passports."

"Spooky as in scary?" I asked.

"No, spooky as in spies. You know, undercover."

"These people have had practice. The Catholic Church created false identities and papers for the Nazis to get them to where they were going. I suppose it's nothing for the Jews to do the same for us."

"Funny, the nuns at Saint James never taught us any of that," noted Lefty.

"The Catholics thought the Jews were the killers of Jesus. They felt the Nazis were paying the Jews back for killing their Savior."

"Where's the Love?" laughed Lefty. "By the way, why did Janet ask if I could snow ski?"

"Can you?" I asked.

"I've been to Tahoe a few times with some chicks. I got down the hill, but it wasn't pretty."

"That's what I thought. We're going to start our search in this ski resort town. We'll mingle with the crowd to get the feel of the place. We'll act like stupid tourists, and Francois and the Jewish underground will guide us along."

Lefty put his hands behind his head and stretched with a big smile on his face, "This is the shit I was made for!"

"It might be the shit that gets you killed," I remarked.

Lefty laughed and slapped me on the back, "Think of the money, Tone."

Draining my glass, I said, "Yeah, think of the money."

Chapter 28

I sat alone nursing a Bloody Mary while I waited for breakfast at the Gran Estamplaza Berrini Hotel in Sao Paulo, Brazil. The Gran Estamplaza Hotel is centered in the high-rise hotel district, surrounded by upscale nightlife establishments. Brazilian pop music played until the early morning hours. It wasn't by chance that the Israeli consulate was in the back half of the building on Rúa James Joule.

Lefty and I met clandestinely with two Israelis the night before at the Gauguin club across Rúa Arizona, from the hotel. The purpose of the meeting was to formulate a plan of action after opening an account at the Faria Lima Financial Center.

Lefty lit a cigarette as he sat down at the breakfast table. A middle-aged man in a black tuxedo played soothing music on the grand piano in the corner.

Lefty eyed the piano player, "I wonder if he'd play Jazz?"

"I'm sure he would for a tip," I answered.

Lefty beckoned the waiter and pointed to the Bloody Mary, "I'll have what he has.' He handed the waiter ten dollars. "Ask the maestro to play some mellow jazz?"

The waiter approached the piano player, slipped the ten dollars into his coat pocket, and whispered into his ear. The piano player looked at Lefty, nodded, and transitioned into Eddie Harris.

The waiter brought Lefty his drink and laid an envelope before me. Eyeing the envelope on the table, I opened it with the butter knife. It read:

Dear Mr. LeGrand,

Your 10:30 a.m. meeting with Mr. Gabriel Mendes is at Faria Lima Financial Center, Ave Faria Lima 3400, Suite 562. At 10 a.m., a car and driver will pick you up in front of the hotel. As instructed, I have 10,000 USD in 100-dollar bills for a deposit in the Adrian account.

Thank you.

I looked at my watch. It was 8:30. I felt the money belt around my waist.

"What are you going to order for breakfast?" I asked Lefty.

"I'm ordering a good old American breakfast: sausage, eggs, and hash browns."

"I don't think they have it. The closest thing is what I ordered, Bife à Cavalo."

"What's that?" asked Lefty.

"Steak and eggs with asparagus and cherry tomatoes on the side."

"Asparagus!" questioned Lefty. "I'll need another Bloody Mary before I have asparagus for breakfast."

I laughed and then rechecked my watch.

"What did you think about those two Jewish guys we met at the sex club last night?" asked Lefty.

They were Israelis," I mentioned.

"What's the difference? They look the same to me."

"The difference is they are citizens of Israel. What I think about them is I'm glad they're on our side."

"Not that I'm complaining, but don't you think it was strange to meet in a sex club."

"I guess there would have been plenty of distractions if someone had tried to listen in."

Lefty smiled and nodded his head, then checked his watch. " It's almost time for the games to begin."

I glanced at my watch, drank the last of my bloody Mary, and then beckoned the waiter for a refill.

Chapter 29

At 10:30, I stood on the curb in front of the hotel, a canvas briefcase dangling from my right hand, waiting for the driver. This was a one-man job. A riviera blue BMW 501 opened the passenger-side window in front of me.

The driver leaned over, "Mr. LeGrand?"

I shook my head, yes. The driver came around and opened the rear door. In the back seat, I fingered the money belt around my middle.

It was four blocks from the financial center. The driver turned down the alley to the VIP entrance. He knocked, then opened the car door for me to get out.

A man stood at the open door with his hand out. We shook hands as I entered. "Mr. LeGrand, I'm Gabriel Mendes. I hope you are having a pleasant stay in Sao Paulo?"

"I am. Thank you."

"Will you be staying long?"

"Unfortunately, I will fly back to San Francisco as soon as our transaction is complete."

"I'm sorry to hear that," said Mendes as they entered the elevator. He pushed the fifth-floor button.

"San Francisco is a beautiful place. I've been there twice," he continued.

"Business or pleasure," I asked.

"Business. I met with Robert LeGrand, and he is your?" he questioned.

"My uncle," I lied.

"I see. We thought Miss Janet would be coming."

"She would've, but she is busy with the changing of the guard. She sends her respects."

"Makes perfect sense," concurred Mendes.

On the fifth floor, Mendes ushered me into his office. A cushioned chair stood at the business side of the desk.

"Please have a seat." invited Mendes as he rounded the desk and sat down.

"I have the papers ready to sign, with account numbers. From what I understand, the Adrian account will be the heading. Is that correct?"

"Yes."

"You have your passport, I take it?"

I said nothing, but took the passport from my briefcase and handed it to Mendes.

Opening the passport, Mendes studied the picture, "I didn't know Mr. LeGrand had any nephews."

I cocked my head, raised an eyebrow with a slight smile, and pointed to the passport.

Mendes kept going back and forth between the passport and my face. His demeanor had a disbelieving look.

I reached into my briefcase and took out a letter, "I suppose you'll need this," then handed it to Mendes.

Unfolding the letter, Mendes read:

To whom it may concern,

I, Janet LeGrand, give my cousin, Tony LeGrand, Passport Number 4286687, all authority to conduct business at the Faria Lima Financial Center in the name of LeGrand Galleries.

He has all the rights as if I were there myself.

Signed,

Janet LeGrand

Under her signature was a stamp signed by her attorney and notary public.

Mendes laid down the letter, opened the passport, and wrote down the passport number on one of the forms.

"If you will sign here, Mr. LeGrand."

After signing, I took the money from the belt and placed it on the desk.

Mendes stood up and offered his hand, "Thank you very much, Mr. LeGrand. My secretary will show you out."

"Aren't you going to count it?" I asked.

"No need for that. Have a pleasant flight."

Chapter 30

Lefty and I were not boarding our flight back to San Francisco. We checked in at Sao Paulo Guarulhos Airport and left the ticket counter carrying a small travel bag.

"See those two Nazi goons following us?" asked Lefty.

"I saw them the minute we entered the airport. The guy on the right was my driver to the bank. They want us to know we're watched."

"If they follow us into the head, we're fucked."

"Play it by the numbers," I coached.

We entered the men's room, where two men, Jewish underground, wore identical clothes as we did. They were in stalls one and three. I cleared my throat three times, then entered stall two. But Lefty had a problem. Stall four was occupied, so Lefty faked hand washing until it opened. Finally, a big fat guy came out. He wore sweatpants and a dirty white T-shirt.

As he entered, you could hear under his breath, "Jesus, the fucking guy didn't even flush the toilet."

Lefty closed the door, changed his clothes, and slid his travel bag under the divider to his accomplice in stall three.

I quickly changed clothes from my travel bag. My Israeli accomplice exchanged bags under the stall divider. In the bag was my original passport, stamped by the Brazilian Alfandega. Thanks to the Jewish underground, I was free to cross the border into Argentina under my own name.

The Israeli accomplice in stall one loudly cleared his throat, the prearranged sign to leave. They waited by the door; they didn't exit the men's room until two women started a fight up the hall. The two Nazis who followed them watched the fight, turned back in time to see the Israeli accomplices round the corner on their way to the gate. The ruse worked momentarily as the men followed them to the departure gate.

At the gate, the Nazi followers realized they were deceived and quickly ran back down the hall and looked for us. But it was too late.

Francois waited in a white Ford van out front in the loading zone. We drove away from the airport. It would take the next three days to reach San Carlos Bariloche, thirteen hours to travel to the Argentina border, crossing at Puerto Iguazu, giving time for the Nazi followers to get the word out to be on the alert.

Chapter 31

The white Van arrived at the border town of Foz de Iguaçu. The sun's rays peeked over the trees as we exited Route 469 via a roundabout to Route 12. We had to check out of Brazil before they entered Argentina. Francois stopped at a kiosk, where a Brazilian customs official approached the van.

"Papeis de viagem," he demanded.

"What'd he say?" asked Lefty.

"He wants your passport and visa," answered Francois.

Francois handed our papers to the official. After the official studied the passports, he stamped and signed them and did the same for the visas.

The official started to get up and sat back down. He opened the passports, looked toward the van, and picked up the phone. He dialed and leafed through the passports while he talked. He hung up the phone and quickly stood and gathered the paperwork.

He handed the passports and visas to Francois, "Voc pode ir."

Lefty asked as we left the checkpoint, "What the fuck was that about?"

"I don't know," I answered.

Francois kept his thoughts to himself.

When we crossed the border over the Iguazu River on the Tancredo Neves Bridge, we were the only car on the road as we entered the Argentina customs checkpoint. The Argentine customs official directed us where to park, then told us to leave the van and led us into an office where another customs official was seated behind a desk.

In perfect English, he said, "Passports and visas, please."

He received the passports and pointed to a bench beside the side wall. "Have a seat," he commanded.

The official compared the passport pictures of each of us sitting on the bench, then looked at Francois. "Mr. Meyer, you are French. Have you been to Argentina before?"

"Oui, I am French, and no, I haven't been to Argentina."

The official opened a folder and picked up a piece of paper, "I have a list of names here. Francois Meyer from Marseille is on the list. Can you tell me why your name would be on this list?"

"I have no idea why Francois Meyer would be on a list. I have no idea what the list is for."

"Mr. Meyer, this is a list of suspected terrorists."

Lefty and I looked at each other, realizing this was trouble.

Francois said, "I have no idea what you are talking about. There are lots of Francois Meyers in France. I am here to go skiing with my friends. Now, if you return our papers, we can get going."

The official sat calmly, pulling a photo from the folder and holding it up. "Do these other Francois Meyers look like this?"

Francois leaned back up against the wall.

A tall German-looking man wearing a dark pinstripe suit entered the office from a side door. He approached the official, leaned down, whispered in his ear, turned, and left.

The official placed the photo and list in the folder, closed it, and put it in the drawer. He then stamped, dated, and signed each passport.

He pushed them to the front of his desk and looked up, "You are free to go."

None of us spoke until we cleared the border crossing compound.

"What do you think? That was weird," said Lefty.

"This is no longer a clandestine operation," I answered. "It's full-on frontal combat. They are out to get us, maybe even kill us."

Francois drove quietly for a while, then said, "They are using us to expose the Jewish underground operating in this region to bring the Nazi murderers to justice. We have been set up from the very beginning."

"There are only six of us who know anything about this. One of us is the snitch," blasted Lefty.

"Maybe you," responded Francois.

"Bullshit, man! I'm in it purely for the money," yelled Lefty.

"Calm down, Lefty, we're in a world of shit. We must think this through," I demanded.

"I'll calm down if Frenchy lays off his bullshit. If this Hiney operation is compromised by the Krauts, we must produce another plan."

"Oui, that is true," Francois responded. "It might be best if we split up."

"Great idea when you are the one with the van. What are me and Tony supposed to do, get out and walk?"

"Damn it, Lefty, cool it," I said, opening a map. "The next large town is Posadas. It's big enough to hide in, hole up, and look for other options. It might be best to ditch this big white van and look for other ways to travel."

"How do you plan to get lost in this town, Posadas?" Lefty sneered.

I looked at the map. "There is a National University of Misiones. We go there and mingle with the students, lay low, and go from there," I said.

Lefty looked at me, turned his eyes to the road, and raised his eyebrows. " That's a good idea—university, young girls, great."

I asked the Frenchman, "What do you think, Francois?"

"Oui," he answered.

Chapter 32

Students mingled around as we exited the van in the university parking lot. Next to the van, a young lad threw his leg over a Cofersa 200 JM motorcycle.

As he was ready to start the motorcycle, I faced the lad and raised my arm, "Perdoneme, hablas Inglesa?"

"Yes. How can I help you?" he answered politely.

"My sister is a student here. She told us to meet her in the lounge. Could you tell us where we can find it?"

"There is no lounge on campus. Most students meet in the Vela Club around the corner."

"Nice motorcycle you have there," interrupted Lefty.

"Thank you. My family has a dealership."

"Really!" I said, a light going off in my head. "Does your family take in trades?"

With our new Cofersa bikes, we headed south on the outskirts of Posadas. Our destination was the Gran Hotel Viena on the shores of Laguna Mar Chiquita. We learned from the meeting at the Gauguin Club that Hotel Viena was a known hangout of Hitler and Eva Braun. It was a risky move, but if Eva had been there, it would make our mission easier.

After a full day's ride, we checked into Hotel Viena. Our rooms were on the second floor, looking over the lagoon. The hotel, built in 1945, had the trappings of European opulence, with elevators and air conditioning. The occupants spoke German, and a smattering of swastikas decorated the walls.

In the dining room, we looked over the menu, "This place is a throwback," commented Lefty. "It looks like Hitler could come marching in any minute."

I figured the direct approach was the best. When the waiter came to the table to take their order, I looked at him and asked, "Is Eva Braun here at the moment?"

The waiter laughed, "You are seeking someone who doesn't exist. People come asking the same question. I can assure you she is not here."

A young woman sat alone at the corner table, sipping cognac and smoking a cheroot. She overheard the conversation, glanced at us, and then lingered until we finished our meals. She followed me at a distance and approached as I unlocked the door to my room.

"I heard your conversation that you're looking for Eva Braun."

"Yes, I am. It's important that I find her."

"Does it have something to do with the Adrian account?"

I released my fingers from the key and faced her, "How'd you know about that?"

The girl handed me a note. *If you are going to Bariloche, go to the Stag restaurant and ask for a man named Bender. Give him this note. He can help you. I must tell you your French friend is in danger. Bender can also help him in his quest, but he must be careful.*

"Who are you?"

"It's best you don't know for now, but we'll meet again," she said as she turned and left without looking back.

I tossed and turned, unable to sleep, as I thought of this mystery woman.

I finally dozed off at 2 am and had a horrible dream. Chased by a pack of vicious German Shepherds, my only escape was to make it over a tall brick wall. My arms and legs felt weighed down, so I could barely run. I hung from the top of the wall and struggled to raise my arms; the dogs began to tear into my flesh.

I woke up, reaching for the top of the wall that wasn't there. Sweating profusely, I wiped my face, the dream vivid in my mind.

It was dark outside. Rattled by the dream, I gathered my belongings and stuffed them into my backpack. I woke up the others.

"We've got to move. We're in great danger here."

"Jews have always been in great danger," responded Francois.

"God damn," said Lefty. "Can't we wait to get a cup of coffee?"

"We'll get some down the road. Come on, gather your gear. We've got to go!"

Down the stairs in the lobby, the receptionist was asleep in a chair behind the counter. Quietly, we placed the room keys on top of the rent and went outside. We strapped the backpacks on the bikes and silently pushed them down the road for a clean getaway.

The receptionist awoke and found the keys and payment on the counter. He picked up the phone and dialed.

Cool air chilled our faces, and we raced down the road too early for morning traffic. We arrived at El Tio feeling safe enough to pull over for breakfast at dawn. The only place open was the small cafe, *Aldecna's*.

"Jesus, I thought you were never going to stop," spouted Lefty.

"We had to make some distance from Miramar," I answered, lowering the kickstand on my bike.

Francois remained on his bike, checking out the surroundings. "I assume we are heading for *Bariloche*," he asked.

"That's right," I answered. "The girl in the hotel told me to go to the *Stag Restaurant* and ask for a guy named Bender."

"Who was that chick?" asked Lefty.

"I don't know, but she knew about the Adrian account and said that Francois was in deep sh.t."

Lefty asked, "Can we trust her?"

"I don't know, but do you have any other ideas?" I answered.

"How far is it to Bariloche?" asked Francois.

I looked at the map. "Eighteen hours, as far as I can guess."

The coffee shop's early morning crowd, busy with conversation, became quiet when I entered.

I approached the counter and ordered three coffees and an apple pie.

The patrons continued to stare.

I paid the lady and took our breakfast outside.

I passed out the pie and said, "If we get split up, we're on our own to get to Bariloche."

The patrons continued to watch through the window, asking each other if they knew these strangers.

"How do we get there?" mumbled Lefty with a mouthful of pie.

I looked at the map, "Go north to 40. It will get you there."

"North to 40," swallowed Lefty.

We headed west as patrons ran outside to watch until we were out of sight.

We rode together to Cordoba and then took the ring road around the second-largest city in Argentina. Forty miles out, we traveled the winding road to the upper Pampas, which has a desert landscape.

From Beasley to Monte Coman was 150 miles of straight desert road. We opened the throttle on the bikes as the miles ticked away. I, in the lead, noticed a red biplane making a banking turn coming straight at us. It raced past so low I could feel the rush of air overhead. At first, I thought it was a weekend pilot having fun until it made a wide turn and came at us again. This time, I noticed white swastikas painted in black circles on the wings. It made another sweeping turn and landed on the road.

We slowed to a stop as the plane taxied toward us. I yelled over the noise, "This is too weird. Let's split up across the desert to ditch this plane."

I looked toward the Andes Mountain range pointing to a large snow capped peak. "Make that mountain your reference point. Get off the road when you hit Highway 40, and head south. We'll try to hook up somewhere down the road. If not, we'll meet up at the hotel in Bariloche.

Now take off!"

We took off in different directions. I went north and the other two in a southerly direction. The plane took off, making wide circles as it followed the dust trails of the bikes. Two lines of bullets splattered the earth on each side of my bike as the plane came up from behind. As it flew overhead, it rocked its wings side to side. If there was any doubt in my mind, I knew now this game was for real.

I ran hard over the desert floor and watched the mountain peak. After five miles in the open desert, I encountered a north-south country road. I checked the sky. There was no red biplane flying around. I took a chance and turned south. Up ahead, a tall radio tower signaled a town nearby. On the outskirts was a small airstrip. Arriving closer, I recognized the red biplane with people pushing the plane into a metal hanger.

I wanted to know who these people were. Laying the bike down off the road, I ran to the back of the hanger. Voices echoed inside. One voice sounded familiar, the voice of a woman. I peeped through a small hole; it was the girl from the hotel. They spoke German. In the little German I knew, I recognized "Mutter," meaning mother and one word came in loud and clear: "Eva."

I thought, *could she be Eva Braun's daughter?*

I was compelled to confront her and find the underlying cause of her involvement when a black car drove up, and three large men exited.

The biggest of the three greeted the woman, "Hallo Ursula."

Where did I hear that name? Those three men would be more than I could manage.

I lay still as they got in the car and drove off. I cautiously entered the resort village of Lujan. One large complex had a casino. Because of the number of vehicles in the parking area, it was doing robust business. In Portes-cochere, there was a black car. The girl, now called Ursula, walked up the stairs to the entrance with two men.

I entered the casino, and the noise from the slot machines was deafening. Past the slot machines, the gambling hall opened with blackjack, roulette, craps, and poker tables. Lost in the crowd, I looked for the threesome. At the far end, there was a bar and buffet. I moved in for a better view and stopped at the craps table, pretending to watch the dice. I spotted them at the buffet filling their plates. They sat at the bar and ordered a beer.

Ursula excused herself and walked around the buffet table to a hallway. I circled to the left and watched her. Down the hall, she entered the women's lounge. This was my chance, so I followed her in.

She stood in front of the mirror and turned when I entered.

"What are you doing here?" she squealed.

"You're Ursula, the daughter of Eva Braun."

"Do you know how much danger you are in!?" she frantically queried.

I ignored the question, "Do you know your half-sister Janet LeGrand is being blackmailed by the Nazis to keep the Adrian account open?"

"I don't know anything about a half-sister. You've got to get out of here."

"I'm not going anywhere until you tell me where to find your mother."

"My mother! You are crazy. I've done all I can do for you. You'd be dead in minutes if they knew we were here talking. They don't care who dies. It's all about the party, the Reich. They are psychopaths. I'm sick of it. I want out!"

"Why did you buzz us in that red plane, trying to kill us?"

"I can't explain things to you. You must leave, go to the Stag, and meet Bender. It's your only hope," she pleaded.

"How can I trust you?"

"All I'd have to do is scream, and you'll be dead."

I paused, stared at her pleading face, turned, and walked out, going down the hall to a side exit. I checked the gas gauge on the motorcycle. I needed gas.

Chapter 33

I filled the tank and took the first road south. Two hours later, I passed a large tree with a Cofersa motorcycle next to it. Lefty sat leaning against the tree, asleep. The noise of my bike woke him up.

Surprised at him sitting there, I asked, "How in the hell did you get here?"

"I forgot those numbers you told me; I drove south until I ran out of gas."

I shook my bike and opened the gas cap. "I've got three-quarters of a tank. I'll give you half. Hopefully, that will get us to a gas station."

I separated the gas line from the carburetor, "Do you know what happened to Francois?"

"No, he took off like a bat out of hell. Seemed like he knew where he was going," answered Lefty.

Transferring gas to my canteen cup, "I ran into that girl again."

"You did! How did that happen?"

"She was in that plane that buzzed us. I passed an airstrip, saw them putting the plane away, and followed them to a casino. I confronted her when she went to the head."

"Wow, what a crazy deal. This whole fucking thing is crazy."

I restored the fuel line, "Are you sorry you came along yet?"

"Hell no! Who else gets to ride a bike in the outback of Argentina chased by Nazis?"

I threw my leg over the bike and turned the key, "Good attitude. Another thing…" as I kicked the start pedal.

"What's that?" asked Lefty.

My bike idling, "I'm pretty sure she's Eva Braun's daughter."

"Oh fuck!" exclaimed Lefty. "That means she's Janet's sister."

"Small world. Come on, let's ride," I commanded.

Chapter 34

Francois knew where he was going. He took the back roads to Rio Cuarto, ditched his bike, and bought an overnight train ticket to Bahia Blanca. The train went to the harbor district. He walked the mile and a half to the industrial area, looking for Lonera Manos's upholstery shop on Pedro Pico Street.

Jacob Gorman, the owner, wore a yarmulke on the back of his balding head. He was a relative of Robert Gorman's from New York. Robert gave Francois this address if he needed assistance. Francois needed help.

He entered the shop and stood there, taking in the surroundings.

Jacob recognized a fellow Jew and addressed him in Yiddish, "Hello, how can I help you?"

Francois slightly bowed and answered in Yiddish, "My name is Francois Meyer. Robert Gorman from New York gave me your address."

Jacob, a member of the Jewish Underground, knew this was not a casual visit and invited Francois into his office.

"Are you familiar with the Adrian account?" asked Francois.

"Yes, Mr. Meyer, I have been in contact with Robert recently and understand the situation."

"I'm traveling with two goyim who are seeking to contact Eva Braun to close the Adrian account network. We work together. I want to bring my parents' killer to justice.

"The man you seek to bring to justice is named Bender. You can find him at the Stag Restaurant in Bariloche."

"That's interesting. A woman my goyim friend met in Mira Mar told us that Mr. Bender could help us."

"That woman was probably Ursula Hitler. Before Hitler died in 1963, he and Eva lived in an estate named Inalco up Lake Nahuel Huapi from San Carlos de Bariloche. Eva gave birth to a daughter in 1938, raised by Eva's parents. She didn't meet her parents until 1945 in Argentina. Eva got bored and left Hitler, then moved to Neuquen with Ursula. They're guarded very closely by the organization. From what we understand, both want to be free from watchful eyes. Ursula is a bit more outspoken. I will tell you Bender is a dangerous man."

"Why would she send us to him?" asked Francois.

"She is young and impetuous, easily manipulated by Nazi groups. If your friends think he's an ally they are dangerously mistaken, rushing towards their deaths. Someone should warn them."

"Warn them!" exclaimed Francois. "I've no idea where they are. We scattered when buzzed by an airplane. They're on motorcycles heading south for Bariloche."

"You were separated two days ago near Cordoba?"

"Oui," answered Francois.

"Bariloche is a full three-day drive from there. They should arrive tomorrow or the next day. Where were you to meet them?"

Taking a note out of his shirt pocket. "A hotel, Cacique Inacayal," he answered.

"I know the place. It's a spa on the lake. We can catch the train and be there by tomorrow night."

Chapter 35

Buck sat in first class on the Pan Am flight when it landed in Buenos Aires. He went through customs, gathered his luggage, and hailed a taxi.

"Embajada Americana," he told the driver.

His first stop was to visit his old Marine buddy, Master Sergeant Wendell Shannon, the head of Marine security at the U.S. Embassy. Shannon, from Oklahoma, was tall and lanky and talked like he had a mouth full of marbles.

"What brings you down here? I heard you were still with the agency," asked Wendell.

"I am, and I'm down here on a mission, Wendell."

"The Last time you were here, you were looking for Hans Kemmler, Hitler's special weapons expert. Did you ever find him?"

"I can't answer that, but I found out he was on the list for *Operation Paperclip*. He caused the death of tens of thousands of slaves from the concentration camps to dig underground factories. He should have been hanged, but the Western nations gave him a free pass if he would turn over his secrets."

"What mission are you on now?"

"It's a bit complicated. It might take me a while to explain."

"That's all right, Buck. As you see, I don't have much to do unless somebody attacks the Embassy; I don't foresee that happening for the next hour or so."

Buck nodded, "I'm assigned to collaborate with a company selling art worldwide. They sold stolen art for the Nazis…."

Wendell sat patiently listening while Buck told him the story.

"That's interesting, Buck. Those rumors of Hitler and Eva living down here go deeper than one would think. How can I help you?"

"We sent two boys to stir things up to see who's at the bottom of the pot. Unfortunately, they are expendable."

"Usually, we recommend American tourists check in with the Embassy. But if they're on a clandestine operation, they would want to be under the radar."

"I know your security clearance is still active, or you wouldn't be working here," said Buck.

Wendell shook his head. "Yes, it's good for the next three months. After that, I'm retiring and moving to Louisiana to fish the bayous for the rest of my life," he added.

"I hate to break up your retirement plans, but I'd like you to come with me to ski on the slopes above San Carlos de Bariloche."

"San Carlos de Bariloche," answered Wendell. "I've been meaning to get out that way. Sure, Buck, I'll go with you. You up for a steak dinner tonight?"

That'd be great. I'll fill you in on the rest."

"I'll meet you in Santos Manjares on Paraguay Street at seven," instructed Wendell.

Chapter 36

Lefty and I entered the Cacique Inacayal Hotel and Spa on Lake Nahuel Huapi. It was hard to believe we were in Argentina, not the Swiss Alps. Blonde, blue-eyed girls dressed in ski apparel lounged around the reception area.

"Has Francois Meyer checked in?" I asked the receptionist.

Checking the ledger. "No, Sir. We have no quest by that name."

"If he checks in, could you please give him this note," handing a sealed envelope to her.

"Of course, Sir. You say you'll be staying for three days?"

"For now. Does the concierge book skiing excursions?"

"Yes. You get a 10% discount on lift tickets."

Great!" I answered. One last question: Could you direct us to the Stag Restaurant?"

The receptionist placed a map on the counter and pointed out the Stag. "Do you have transportation?"

"Yes, we do," I answered.

"Then no problem," and handed me the keys. "Room 307 and 309."

On the way up the stairs, "Hey Tone, did you check out those blondes hanging around?"

"I'm not blind, Dude."

Opening their connecting room doors, Lefty threw in his pack: "I'm going down to the bar and washing down this road dust."

"I'm going to take a shower first; I'll meet you down there."

Lefty hesitates, "They did tell us to mingle, didn't they?"

"That they did."

When I got to the bar, Lefty had three hot-looking blondes standing around him. His arm draped over the shoulder of one, entertaining her with his wit.

"Hey, Tone, let me introduce you to my friends," he said as he pointed to Gertrude. This is Hilda."

"No, I'm Gertrude," she laughed.

Hilda smiled at Lefty, "I'm Hilda," she corrected.

The girl with his arm around, "Let's not forget Bambi. Who could forget Bambi?" he laughed.

"We're talking about hitting the slopes tomorrow. Are you up for that?" Lefty continued.

I nodded my head with raised eyebrows, "Why not?" Then beckoned for the bartender.

"Jack Daniels on the rocks," I ordered.

"Sorry, Sir, we don't have Jack Daniels. Will *Vat 69* work?"

Frowning, "Yes, that will do. Refresh these girls' wine glasses."

It was a fun night with laughter, bumps, and grinds. The girls enjoyed our company. It got late, and even Lefty was road-weary and ready for bed.

I waved over the bartender, "I'll take the bill."

The bartender pointed to the door, "It's already been taken care of by that lady."

Ursula stood by the door. Our eyes met. She turned and left. I rushed to the door to catch her, but she was gone.

Back at the bar, "Do you girls know Ursula?" I frantically asked.

They looked at each other and laughed. Bambi said, "You guys are so much fun. See you tomorrow at the lodge at eleven o'clock."

With a kiss and a hug, they waved goodnight.

"What was that about?" asked Lefty.

"Ursula set up those girls to keep us on a string."

"What should we do about it?"

"Meet them at the lodge tomorrow at eleven," I answered.

Chapter 37

The train pulled into Bariloche station at 11:15. Jacob and Francois hailed a cab for the Cacique Inacayal Hotel. Buck and Wendell landed at Bariloche Airport at 11:25 and booked a room at the Cacique Inacayal Hotel as well.

Jacob and Francois got there first. The receptionist looked at Francois's passport.

"Mr. Meyer, you have a note from Mr. Tony Taylor."

Opening the envelope, *"Francois the situation is unsure, not sure who to trust. Don't do anything until we hook up."*

Francois pondered the note and then passed it to Jacob.

"Your rooms are 218 and 220," instructed the receptionist.

Chapter 38

I nursed a Bloody Mary on the Pire Hue Ski Lodge deck when I noticed the girls in front of the lodge. I waved and yelled to get their attention. They smiled and waved, and it began to snow.

"So, we're not going skiing, and you're not planning to get laid?" asked Lefty.

"Not if I can help it. I want to find out who these girls are and their relationship with Ursula."

"How do you plan to do that?"

"I'm going to come right out and ask them. They won't want to ski with us when I'm finished."

Mimosas in hand, the girls came out on the deck wearing big smiles. I stood to greet them as Lefty gathered three extra chairs and placed them around the table. Before they sat, there were hugs and kisses.

Gertrude sat down and asked, "Have you been here long?"

"Not long," I answered. Then I cut to the chase, "Before we go on, I must ask again. What is your relationship with Ursula? She is Eva Braun's daughter, and I have an urgent message for her."

The girls looked at each other and laughed when Hilda asked, "I thought we were going skiing?"

In a forceful tone, "I'm not going skiing. I need some answers."

"We have to go skiing," said Hilda. "There is someone wanting to meet you on the slopes."

Chapter 39

Buck and Wendell opened their suitcases on the beds. Each took out a 1911 Colt 45. They loaded magazines in the handles and pulled back the slides, placing a round in the chamber. Adding silencers to the barrel, they placed their weapons in their shoulder holsters.

"What's the first thing we must do?" asked Wendell.

"We need to find out what those boys are up to," said Buck, looking out the window. "Wendell, come look at this."

"Yeah, what's up?"

"See those two men standing on the porch?"

"The tall guy wearing black?' asked Wendell.

"That's Francois Meyer. I don't know who the other man is. Do you?"

"Never seen him before. Looks like they're waiting for a ride."

"Let's see if we can find those other two boys."

On a hunch, Buck went to the concierge desk, "I'm looking for a couple of friends who I believe are out skiing. Did they book an excursion with you?"

"What are their names?" asked the concierge.

"Mr. Tony Taylor and Lefty Jackson."

"Yes, they booked a Pire Hue ski resort tour this morning."

Chapter 40

At the top of the ski run, the girls struggled to get Lefty's skis on. They laughed and giggled, teased, and called him funny names. They started down the slope. Lefty got thirty yards and took his first dive. The girls circled around him, laughing, and got him back on his skis.

Hilda turned to me, "You go on. We'll work with Lefty."

I started down the 2-mile run. My senses were alert. The fresh snow held my concentration until I sensed someone coming up behind me. Turning hard, I dug into the edge of my skis and stopped, allowing the person to pass. A woman skied by, her face covered with a scarf. She looked at me and gestured to follow. I hesitated; she turned and stopped forty yards ahead, looked back, and gestured again. I straightened my skis, pushed off with the poles, and followed her through the tall pine forest. After a quarter mile, she came to a snow-covered meadow. In the middle was a cabin, smoke billowed from the chimney. She was taking off her skis when I caught up to her.

"Please, come inside," she ordered, entering the warm, cozy cabin.

Closing the door behind me, a wood stove crackled away with a tea kettle steaming from the spout. A table with a tea setting for two stood on the brightly finished wood floor. A sliced chocolate Black Forest cake in the middle. A cuckoo clock came to life on the far wall. It was 12 o'clock.

The woman stoked the stove and stood up, unwrapping her scarf from her face.

"Would you like a cup of tea?" invited Ursula.

Chapter 41

Francois and Jacob entered the upholstery shop on Marino Street, greeted in Yiddish by Ruben, Jacob's brother. The shop was a front for seeking war criminals. Bariloche was where the action was.

"Bender's former name was Jacques Pernice," explained Ruben. "When he first arrived, he assigned the boat driver to deliver people and supplies to Hitler in Inalco. He became good friends with Eva and her daughter. When Eva left Inalco, he helped her and Ursula when they moved to Neuquen. What makes him so dangerous is that he was fiercely loyal to Hitler, and now that Hitler is dead, he is fiercely loyal to Eva. If he feels something is not right, he shoots first and doesn't even think about asking questions."

"Does Ursula know this about him?" asked Francois.

"No. Those women were heavily sheltered, and he can be incredibly charming."

"She told us to meet him at the Stag Restaurant."

"He frequents the Stag but still runs the boat out to Inalco to deliver supplies for the caretakers. I say caretakers; they are former SS henchmen."

"Sounds like we're Daniel in the lion's den," stated Francois.

"More like the wolf's lair," countered Ruben. "But let's see what Adonai will do."

"My two goyim friends are here to contact Eva."

"It's not going to be easy. Like I said, he doesn't ask questions."

"Where should we start?" asked Francois.

"Let's go have lunch at the Stag to see who comes and goes," suggested Ruben.

"I'd take off those Yarmulkes if I were you," warned Francois.

Chapter 42

Lefty sat tied to a chair in a room, his bloodied face hanging down on his chest. A single light bulb hung from the ceiling, exposing the whitewashed block walls.

A bucket of chilly water was thrown in his face; he jerked up.

"One more time, what's your business here in Bariloche?" demanded Bender.

"I told you, man, pick up chicks and go skiing."

A fist smashed against his head, causing his ears to ring as his head jolted.

"Bullshit! What's your interest in Ursula and her mother."

"I don't know what you're talking about," he meekly answered.

Another smash to the head. Lefty was out cold.

Chapter 43

Ursula placed a piece of Black Forest cake in front of me. She asked, "So, what is this? I have a half-sister blackmailed by the Nazis?"

"I think you know a lot more than you're letting on." I answered. "You're aware of the Adrian account."

"I know my father bought art for his collection under what he called the Adrian account."

"He didn't buy art; he stole it from people he sent to the gas chambers."

"Yes, I've heard this before. But it's so crazy how anybody could believe such things. Bender tells me it's propaganda to make my father look bad."

I looked at her in shock, unable to gather my thoughts to respond. How could anybody be so uninformed?

"I don't want to talk about that anymore. You're here because I've talked to my mother and told her about Janet. She said she won't talk to a third party, no matter the issue. She'll only discuss it with Janet herself," said Ursula.

"Janet has to come here?"

"That's right, Mother lives in Neuquen, and she wants her to come there."

"How is she going to do that? She can't go knock on her door."

"I'll take her there, but Mother said no one must know about it. Do you understand what I'm saying?"

After a pause, "Yes, I'll tell her to come, and you take over from there."

Jolted by a loud knock on the door, "Ursula, let me in. It's Hilda!"

Opening the door, Hilda screamed, crying, "They've taken Lefty."

I jumped up, "Who's taken Lefty?!"

"They have!" she cried.

I clamped on my skis, "How do I get to the Lodge?" he asked.

Ursula pointed down the hill, "What are you going to do?" she asked.

I drove ski poles into the snow, "Go find him."

"How are you going to do that?"

"I'm going to start by going to the Stag."

As I gained momentum over the snow, I faintly heard, "Be careful!"

Chapter 44

Fresh snow lay on the ground as Buck and Wendell paid the cabbie in front of the ski resort.

"This isn't going to be easy with the crowd here," mentioned Wendell.

"We'll check out the bar, and if they're not there, go to the ski rental shack and see if they rented skis. If they're on the slope, they'll have to return the skis."

I skied to the shack and didn't notice Buck standing there as I unlatched the skis. I felt a hand on my back, looked up, and Buck smiled at me.

I didn't greet or ask for an explanation why Buck was there when I blurted out, "They captured Lefty. We must find him."

"Who captured him?" questioned Buck.

"I'm pretty sure it was goons sent by this guy named Bender."

"I recognize that name from intelligence briefings," said Wendell.

"Who are you?" I asked, picking up the skis.

"This is Wendell, he's with me."

"How did you find me, and what are you doing here?"

Buck said, "We'll explain that later. Where do you think they took Lefty?"

"I don't know, but I'll start looking at the Stag Restaurant. It's supposed to be where Bender hangs out."

"We'll meet you there. We'll go separately so they won't know we're together. You ask questions, and we'll back you up if there is trouble."

I yelled, "Wait!" and stopped them. "Ursula said her mother would only communicate with Janet directly. Janet must come down here."

It took a moment to sink into Buck's brain before he answered, "We'll work on that later. Right now, let's find Lefty."

Buck and Wendell entered the Stag.

Francois was halfway through his meal, knife and fork in hand, when he looked up and recognized Buck. The other two turned to see what Francois was looking at. Francois looked shocked.

Buck didn't acknowledge Francois, but he felt the 1911 under his coat. He and Wendell sat at the bar.

"What can I get you to drink?" asked the barkeep.

"I'll have water," answered Buck.

"Imperial for me," added Wendell.

When I got to the Stag, I was in a heightened state of anxiety. I lost any cool I had and was ready for combat.

I entered and saw Francois sitting in the corner with two other men.

I rushed to the table and blurted out, "Francois, we're in the shit now, Lefty's been abducted, and we have to find him!"

Totally caught off guard, Francois wiped the crumbs off his lips. He didn't know how to reply and felt exposed in the restaurant.

"Did you hear what I said?" I blurted out again.

Offering me the empty seat, "Oui, please have a seat."

"I'm not sitting down until I find this Bender dude!" I yelled.

The barkeep came up and put his hand on my shoulders, "Can I help you, sir?"

"No, thank you," I answered loud enough for all to hear. "I'm looking for Bender. Do you know where I can find him?"

"Bender? I don't know anybody by that name."

I grabbed the barkeep by the lapels screaming in his face, "You lie, you son of a bitch! You're going to tell me where he is, or I'm going to eat your face off right here and now!!"

The barkeep, too shocked to answer, stood there when Buck and Wendell rushed over and separated us. Forcibly pushing me out the door.

"No need to worry about this fellow," said Buck, looking at the barkeep. "We'll take care of him."

Francois and the two brothers calmly watched this drama unfold. Francois realized the mission would unravel unless they combined forces.

Under his breath, looking down at his food, he uttered, "We're going to have to help him find his friend."

"More than likely, they have him out in the tower," answered Ruben.

"What's the tower?"

"It's a castle-looking tower on a cliff overlooking the lake that guards Hitler's home in Inalco. There is a small garrison there watching for traffic coming their way. From what we understand, there's people there."

"How many do you think?" asked Francois.

"Not sure, but I know they won't be handing out welcome cards, especially if your friend is in there."

"How do we check it out?"

Jacob pondered and broke into the conversation, "We can use kayaks and paddle in to make our attack."

"It's a good idea," returned Ruben. "Except you have a 53-mile paddle before you get there."

"Can we get a boat to get us close?" asked Francois.

"Yes, I can get a boat. Who should go?"

"Us three and Tony and his friends. We'll need five kayaks," answered Francois.

"Why five?" asked Jacob.

"One of us stays with the boat," answered Francois. "And we'll have to go in armed. Do we have weapons?"

"We are the underground. You do know that?"

"Yes of course, stupid question," answered Francois.

Chapter 45

Janet picked up the phone, "Hello."

Henry urged her, "I received a telegram from Buck for you. I'll read it to you."

"What's it got to do with me? I want this whole thing to be over!"

"Listen, Janet, there's no other way!"

After a pause, he read:

I met with the principal's daughter. The principal will deal only with Janet. She must come as soon as possible. I am waiting for your reply. Buck.

"Who's the principal's daughter?" she screamed.

"It's your half-sister."

"Half-sister! I didn't know I had a half-sister!"

"You do now. If you want to bring this whole episode to closure, you'll have to go meet her," said Henry.

"Oh God! That's why we sent Tony down there. He was supposed to figure it out."

"He figured it out, Janet. Now the rest is up to you."

Janet sobbed on the phone, "Oh my God, Henry, when do I have to go?"

"As soon as you get packed. Make sure you bring warm clothes."

"Are you coming with me?"

"Yes, I'll arrange the flight."

Chapter 46

After sunset, in the evening after-glow, a twenty-six-foot Bertram inboard cabin cruiser tied to the dock. Ruben loaded extra cans of gasoline. Buck, Wendell, and I watched as Jacob and Francois approached us, carrying a large suitcase.

Ruben looked up, "We're about ready."

Jacob went aboard and opened the suitcase, exposing four Uzi machine pistols.

"You said you already had weapons," said Jacob looking at Buck and Wendell.

They both nodded.

Behind the Bertram were five kayaks tied in a line. Jacob gathered the group. "We'll tow the kayaks to three miles of the tower, then paddle the rest. We'll find Lefty in the basement. Buck and Wendell will go down and retrieve Lefty. Tony, you, and Ruben stay outside and cover anyone approaching. Francois will stay with the boat. If you hear any shots, race to the tower to get us. Let's get going."

In the darkness, Francois, at the helm, opened the throttle and headed toward the middle of the lake.

Chapter 47

Janet and Henry were late getting to the airport. They ran down and climbed the stairs to the Pan-Am 707 and entered the first-class cabin. In the second row to the right, Mr. Akia Ishikawa sat next to the window, and Michiko Seco was in the aisle. It was an awkward moment.

Settled in the seats two rows back, Janet asked Henry, "What are they doing here?"

"It is strange," answered Henry. "Our first stop is Sao Paulo. Maybe they live there."

"There's got to be more to it than that. I'll bet they had a listening device, and the Nazis put them here to intimidate us."

"Don't overthink it, Janet. It could be purely coincidence."

"Bullshit!" She loudly whispered in his ear. "You always counter whatever I say. I'm telling you there is something to it. What makes you think they live in Sao Paulo in the first place?"

"Conjecture."

"Conjecture! You think you're so goddamn smart. What's conjecture got to do with anything?"

"Lower your voice, Janet. You want the whole plane to think you're crazy?"

"Okay," she answered in a softer tone. "So, what does conjecture have to do with it?"

"They're Japanese working with the Nazis. Sao Paulo has the biggest Japanese population outside of Japan. The Nazis are reestablishing the Fourth Reich in Argentina and Brazil… Conjecture."

"And they happen to be on the same plane we're on."

"That is a bit strange, I will admit," agreed Henry.

Two hours into the flight, Miss Seco bowed slightly before Janet and Henry. "So sorry, Mr. Ishikawa and I will be your guides once we land in Buenos Aires."

Chapter 48

Pitch dark under the overcast sky, there wasn't a breath of wind as the five kayakers rounded the last point of land fifty yards from the tower. As with most well-laid-out plans that go awry, this one was no different. A 40-foot cabin cruiser was idling tied to the dock under the tower.

The kayaks came to a stop unnoticed in the dark. We watched the activity and checked our weapons. Ruben recognized Bender standing in the cockpit, helping two other men lift Lefty aboard.

"I think I can take out the two on the dock," said Jacob under his breath.

"Bullshit," I whispered. "Lefty's too close. We need another plan."

Wendell took command: "They're getting ready to leave, Tony. You, Jacob, and Ruben follow me and disperse. When they leave, we converge on the boat and kill the helmsman. Buck, you stay here and kill anyone left on the dock."

Without time to discuss his plan, Wendell paddled out into the lake.

We hesitated briefly until Buck, with a pistol in hand, commanded, "Get your asses moving!"

The kayaks held back beyond the glow of the dock as we caught up with Wendell.

"Spread out twenty yards apart," he commanded.

"What about Lefty?" I asked again.

"Listen, Taylor, this is the only chance we have. If we miss this opportunity, you'll never see Lefty again."

I felt uneasy, but couldn't produce a better plan and paddled out.

The boat, with Lefty, the helmsman, and another person, left the dock. A red light on the steering station, exposed the helmsman. Lefty was tied up on the floor. Bender steered the boat toward the middle of our flotilla.

Hunkered in the silent darkness, we let the boat pass before firing. Glass shattered from the cabin windows, and splinters of wood flew in every direction from the wood deck house and hull. The head of the figure standing in the cockpit exploded. He fell out of sight. Hearing the shots, Buck fired one round at the lone figure on the dock. The figure fell into the lake, floating face down.

Francois heard the shots and opened the throttle. He raced toward the action, beaming a spotlight from the top of the cabin. When he came upon Buck paddling to join the others, he cut the throttle to reach out and pull Buck aboard.

"Where are the others?"

"Just ahead," Buck directed.

Francois idled forward. The kayaks appeared one by one, positioned next to the boat for boarding, all except Jacob. Ruben had him draped in the middle of his kayak, his face in the water dead. Shot through the heart.

Chapter 49

The Pan Am flight taxied to the Ministro Pistarini terminal twenty miles from Buenos Aires. A black limousine waited on the tarmac. Ursula stood with her arms folded against her chest to keep warm. Mr. Ishikawa negotiated the portable stairs leaning up against the plane. Ursula ran up to him and Miss Seco and gave them prolonged hugs, tears running down her cheeks. Janet and Henry witnessed this emotional reunion as they followed behind.

Miss Seco opened the conversation by saying, "My dear Ursula, let me introduce your sister, Janet, and her brother, Henry."

Ursula stood before Janet reached down and took her hand.

"It's so nice to meet you both. Please come inside the car," she said, ushering them to the open door guarded by the driver.

Crowded together in the back seat, Janet and Henry were speechless. Ursula turned to the driver, spoke in German, and the limousine slowly moved away from the plane.

Henry, curious, "Don't we have to go through customs?"

Ursula smiled, "Yes, of course. We're going to the VIP lounge to be taken care of, as we have refreshments."

Chapter 50

They placed Jacob's body in the cockpit, his lifeless eyes staring at the overcast skies in the early dawn. There was enough light to see smoke pouring from Bender's boat as it tried to make a getaway. Francois opened the throttle, giving chase. As we came alongside, Lefty was at the helm. He raised a machine pistol and started firing.

I yelled, "Lefty! It's us, stop firing!"

Lefty realized his mistake, and dropped the pistol, cut the engines, and fell to the floor, curled up weeping and holding his head.

I jumped aboard the smoking wreck. Lifting Lefty, I held his head against my chest, weeping profusely. The two dead Germans lay in pools of their own blood. Bender's throat slit.

Chapter 51

Sitting next to each other on the train to Neuquen, Ursula held Janet's hand, "I really didn't know who my parents were. I lived with my grandparents. Miss Seco was my nanny. I loved her dearly. Mr. Ishikawa lived next door. He was like an uncle to me. I even called him Uncle. They did everything for me. I found out later that he worked in the Japanese Embassy."

"Did you live in Germany during the war?" asked Janet.

"Yes, we did. We lived in Bamberg. There was no bombing in the area where we lived. In fact, I was very sheltered and never knew a war was happening."

"What about the Holocaust?" questioned Henry. "You must have surely heard of the Holocaust?"

"I don't believe in such things; nobody could be so cruel."

Janet and Henry looked at each other in disbelief. Janet glanced at Miss Seco, staring ahead, not entering the conversation. Mr. Ishikawa sat with his cane between his legs, smiling.

"Do you know why I'm here?" asked Janet.

"Yes, because my mother asked to see you. Tony said you and I were sisters. When I told her about you, she said she had to see you."

"What do you know about the Adrian account?" asked Henry.

"My father bought and sold artwork through this arrangement. I was up at Chiquita Lagoon when Tony was there. Bender called me and told me to contact him; he said he was an art broker, mentioned the Adrian account, and said I was to tell Tony to meet him at the Stag in Bariloche. He told me to ensure I didn't tell him who I was."

Henry couldn't hold back anymore, "This stolen artwork your father was dealing with came from the Jewish people he was sending to the gas chambers. Your sister and I are here to tell your mother that millions of people have died to provide her and you with an income. Your sister's life is in danger if she doesn't keep this arrangement open. This must stop!"

Ursula looked at him blankly, and tears welled up in her eyes. "It's true, it's true. They kept telling me it was a lie, but deep down, I suspected it was true. I didn't want to believe it!" She laid her head on Miss Seco's breast and began to sob. Miss Seco gently stroked her hair.

The train stopped in Neuquen, where a black car waited for them. It stopped at a walled villa where a man opened the gate. The car stopped in front of steps that led to a large wooden double door. A hunched-over Indian housekeeper escorted them to the sitting room lit by standing lamps, warmed by flames leaping in the fireplace. Eva didn't rise from her stuffed chair. A woolen blanket covered her knees as the group gathered around her.

Focusing directly on Janet, "You're Janet," Eva said.

Janet could only nod her head as tears streamed down her cheeks.

Eva reached out and beckoned her to come. As they clasped hands, Eva said, "I'm your mother. You will be safe now. I was young when I met your father and very silly. The times were magical and exciting, but I felt left out and hurt because Adolph had no time for me. Your father was so handsome and charming, so I reached out to him, and we had a moment. I got pregnant and kept it a secret."

"Nobody knew you were pregnant?" Janet asked in disbelief.

"My mother and grandparents knew. I stayed with them until you were born. I contacted your father and told him, and we arranged an adoption."

"But what about Adolph and Alice, who I thought was my mother?" Janet asked again.

"Adolph was totally consumed in politics. I'd go weeks, even months without seeing him. Alice… she never knew. Your father never told her.

He just let her think you were an orphan he learned about on one of his buying trips."

The logic escaped Henry of killing off half the earth so a few could live in luxury. "Mrs. Hitler!" he began, shaking with almost uncontrollable hatred. "For you to be able to sit there and tell us this so casually when it has caused the death, anguish, and misery of millions of people. How you can live with yourself is well beyond my ability to cope or understand! Mrs. Hitler, you must join forces with the civilized world to bring this horrible episode to an end! Help us bring the perpetrators to justice so this will never happen again!"

Henry paused briefly as Eva lowered her eyes from his, then he continued, "Do you understand the gravity of what your people have done?"

She looked into his eyes, speaking softly, "It was the uniforms... the young men looked so handsome and proud. How could we resist the marching, the music, the message of hope? It was so much bigger than us."

"It's all over now." insisted Henry.

"Yes, it's all over now. Adolph is dead, and the organization is nothing but a shell. Trust me, I will do what I can to stop the madness. You have my word on that. I don't want anything to happen to Janet."

Chapter 52

That is how the whole adventure went down.

Back at Tony Nik's after the *San Francisco Herald* reporter left, Jim gave Lefty a beer on the house. Lefty nodded at Jim, then turned to me,

"Tone, I won't join you on your next adventure."

"I wouldn't bet on that."

"How can you say that?"

"No telling what may come up next," I answered, stubbing out my cigarette in the ashtray. "But it's not in your nature to sit things out, especially if money and women are involved."

Lefty downed the last half of his beer, glanced at me from the corner of his eye, and muttered, "Shit."

"See you next week." I said, clapping Lefty on the shoulder.

About the Author

Author Bob Means joined the Marines in the 1960s to escape a troubled childhood. Oblivious to the war in Vietnam, he was soon in the middle of combat, surviving two of the severest operations during the war (Operation Swift and the Tet Offensive). He returned home to struggle with his sanity, suffering from PTSD and an addiction to adrenaline. Bob found relief when he was invited to build an orphanage in Guatemala. This led to a thirty-year adventure as a shelter consultant in overseas disaster relief through a faith-based organization.

His fictional writing is inspired by his travels and the people he met, drawing on their experiences to create his stories. Although his writings are fiction, they are not far from the truth.

He is the author of three books in the Tony Taylor Adventure series and a memoir about the aftermat of the Vietman war.

ALSO BY BOB MEANS

My Soul to Keep, a Marine's Journal After Combat
Stealing Chili Relleno
In Search of Sandino's Gold

www.ingramcontent.com/pod-product-compliance
Lightning Source LLC
Chambersburg PA
CBHW021922170626
46807CB00007B/2945